H04A

ONE TO RIDE
THE RIVER WITH

ONE TO RIDE
THE RIVER WITH

MICHAEL HAMMONDS

DOUBLEDAY & COMPANY, INC.

GARDEN CITY, NEW YORK

1974

ISBN: 0-385-09631-3
Library of Congress Catalog Card Number 74-2717
Copyright © 1974 by Michael Hammonds
All Rights Reserved
Printed in the United States of America

First Edition

For my Grandmother, Olive Holcombe Hammonds
A Westerner

with thanks to Harold Kuebler, Jack Bickham, and Bob Mills

ONE TO RIDE
THE RIVER WITH

ONE

The morning was cold, the wind from the mountains chilled with the threat of snow as Seth Mattick stepped out onto his porch. Pulling on his heavy coat, the old rancher glanced north to a jagged line of peaks. Clouds darkened them, wrapping the high country in winter.

"Damn," the old man grumbled, a frown settling through his leather face. Buttoning his coat, he ambled down the steps and through the scattered light to the barn. Two horses, a dun and a bay, stood in their stalls. Untying them, Seth slapped them down the aisle to the corral. Following, he walked to the door and leaned his long frame against the brace, watching the horses for a moment, smiling.

There was something about them frisking across the corral, steam jutting from their nostrils and trailing behind their tossing heads, that made him forget his troubles for a while. Nate, the dun, came back toward Seth, then stopped, pivoting away again. Seth's smile widened. He was too proud to beg for food. The bay was already at the hay trough next to the barn.

"All right," the old rancher called to them, and was turning back inside when he saw a figure in the ground fog walking up the ranch road. Squinting, Seth tried to make him out, but all he could really be sure of in the poor light was that the visitor was a man.

"What the hell?" he wondered aloud.

At the hay trough the bay nickered impatiently.

"Comin'," Seth said, nodding. He walked back into the barn, lifted a bale of hay from a dwindling stack on the floor, then carried it to a small trap door in the wall. Shoving the door open, the hay trough in the corral was below him.

Taking a pair of cutters from the wall, he clipped the wire holding the hay and rammed it through the door and out into the trough. He hung the cutters back on the wall, then walked back through the barn and out into the yard.

The man had come by the front gate, and Seth could see him better now. Dark-haired, tall, average build, in his late teens or early twenties Seth judged, dressed in a red pile-lined coat, hat, jeans, and hiking boots.

"Morning," the stranger said, smiling as he approached. "Mr. Mattick?"

Seth nodded warily. "That's right. How'd you know my name?"

The stranger gestured over his shoulder. "Your mailbox on the highway."

"What can I do for you?"

The stranger's smile mixed with rue. "Car trouble. Like I said, I saw your box and wondered if I could use your phone. Not a lot of people on that road this time of mornin'."

Seth grinned. "Not a lot of people on it any time." He pointed to the house. "Phone's on the wall just inside the kitchen door there. If it's just a ride you need, I'm goin' in as soon as I grain these horses."

The stranger shook his head. "Afraid it's gonna need a wrecker. Valves, it sounds like."

Seth sighed disgustedly. "Goddamn machines. Wouldn't own one if I didn't have to. Nothin' about this modern age worth a match in a hard wind." His eyes came up to the stranger's and he shook his head, smiling. "Sound like a crotchety old man, don't I? 'Course, your bein' young, I don't imagine you'd agree with grumblin's like that."

The stranger's eyes darkened slightly as if he were remembering something. He nodded vaguely. "Matter of fact, I would." He looked to the house. "In the kitchen you said?"

The old rancher nodded. "Be with you in a minute. There's coffee on the stove, there—" he hesitated. "What is your name, anyhow, son? Always feel lopsided tryin' to talk to someone and not knowin' what to call him."

"Dave McCord," he said, then frowned slightly. "Better get to it."

"Book's right there beside the phone. Go on in," he said, and turned back across the yard to the barn.

Dave McCord watched him for a moment, then, mounting the steps, he went into the house. The warmth felt good and, standing for a moment, Dave rubbed his arms and hands. Looking around, he found that he was standing in a large kitchen-living room. The kitchen area was immediately inside the door, then to the right was a couch, two easy chairs and a fireplace at the far end. On the mantle was a picture of a woman and another of two young men. Above them a rifle hung on pegs. Dave looked back to the telephone on the wall next to the door. The phonebook dangled on a string next to it. Picking up the directory, Dave looked up the number of the only wrecker and dialed it.

"Three Medicine Wrecking Service," a voice rasped over the line, "Bob Sims."

"Mr. Sims," Dave began, "I just had my car quit on me, south of Three Medicine. It's right near the road leading to a man named Mattick's ranch."

"Out by Seth's? Sure. What do you need, a haul in?"

"Yeah. Looks like the valves. I didn't want to drive it any further."

"Good idea," Sims said. "Valves, huh? I can give you a good price on a valve job."

The stranger leaned on the wall. "No need, Mr. Sims."

"You mean you don't want me to fix it?"

"No."

"Well," the man on the telephone stammered, "you're gonna need a car."

"No," the stranger said, "not really. I'll see you later today. I'll sign it over to you for the hauling cost."

"All right," Sims grumbled.

As he started to hang up the phone, Dave heard Sims shout, "Hey, fella! Hey!"

Dave put the phone back to his ear.

"I didn't get your name," Sims said.

"Ahh . . . Martin," he lied, "Dave Martin."

Seth came through the door as McCord hung up. Going to the stove, the old rancher poured two cups of coffee and handed one to the stranger.

"Get hold of 'em?" Seth asked, sipping the hot liquid.

Dave McCord nodded. "Fella named Sims."

"Bob'll do you right." He downed the rest of his coffee. "Best be headin' in."

Dave drained his cup and placed it on the table, then the two men went down the steps around the side of the house to a small garage.

Walking, Dave looked to the peaks.

"Beautiful country," he said.

Seth stopped at the garage door and followed McCord's gaze. "I suppose," he allowed, and began pulling open the door.

Dave looked at him. "You don't sound too fond of it."

The old rancher hesitated, shrugging. "I'm fond enough of it," he said. "Wouldn't be anywhere else. Folks that only see it once in a while tend to think romantic about it." He frowned. "It ain't romantic. No water this summer killed off half my herd, now looks like there's gonna be a helluva snow this winter. I'm gonna have to hire out just to break even or lose this place." He shook his head. "No, son, it ain't romantic, it's just a damn hard land."

Seth got his old pickup running, and a few minutes later the two men were bouncing down the road to the highway. Dave directed Seth to his car, where the young man pulled a pack and a Winchester out of the back seat, put them into the bed of the truck, then climbed back in beside Seth.

"Goin' huntin'?" the old rancher asked.

"You might say that," the young man said.

Nodding Seth rolled the pickup back out onto the blacktop. "Come a long way?" Seth asked.

"A piece." Dave stretched his back. "Feels like I've been driving a month. There a good hotel in Three Medicine?"

Seth grinned. "There's a hotel," he said, "and in this town that's sayin' somethin'."

Dave smiled and looked out the window. "A lot of room for lonesome," he said quietly.

The old rancher looked at him. "Long time since I've heard that. Yeah," he said, nodding, "that's a good way of putting it."

Topping a rise, the town lay stretched out below them.

"Three Medicine." Seth pointed as they began their descent toward it.

Crossing a river bridge, the highway became the main street of the town. Stores and gas stations scattered along the pavement, a residential section to the south, corrals, then pastures lifting to the hills and mountains to the north.

Seth pulled off the road across the wide gravel shoulder in front of a feed store and a grocery, finally pulling up beside a sheriff's car in front of the Pride Restaurant.

Stiffening slightly, Dave kept his eyes on the black and white, getting out slowly, lifting his pack and rifle out of the back.

"Thanks." He nodded to Seth.

"Glad I could do it."

Dave started to turn, then looked back at the old man. "Wouldn't know where I could buy a horse, offhand?"

Seth pointed across the highway. "Same fella that runs the hotel. Bill Edwards. Runs pack trips in the summer." He narrowed his eyes. "Where the hell you headed, anyway?"

"Grass River," Dave answered, shouldering his pack.

Seth blinked. "Grass River? That's a ghost town, son."

"I know." Dave nodded. "Thanks, for the help," he said and, turning, he started across the highway.

In the Pride Restaurant, Sheriff Tom Quade and his deputy Milt Chambers were eating breakfast. Quade, a big, heavystomached man with thinning salt-and-pepper hair, was concentrating on his waffles. His deputy, a thin young man with quick eyes, peered out the window as Seth Mattick and the stranger climbed out of the pickup.

"Ain't never seen him," Chambers commented, leaning on the table, rubbing his hairless chin.

"Who's that?" Quade asked, looking up, sipping his coffee.

"Some fella Seth Mattick just brought into town. Hitchhiker it looks like."

A slight smile touched the sheriff's lips. "Hitchhikers can be a bad bunch," he said.

"Yeah." Chambers nodded, then, realizing the prod, he shrugged. "Just tryin' to keep my eyes open."

Quade's smile widened. "I know," he said, "but you're so damn serious about it, I can't help but josh you."

The deputy surrendered a self-conscious grin. "Guess I am a little eager sometimes."

Quade's eyes moved to the door as Seth came inside. "Damned if it ain't the old man," he said, smiling.

Seth scowled and smiled at the same time. "Watch who you're callin' old," he said, sitting down. "See you're still growin' your belly."

Quade glanced at his stomach and sighed. "Some things are worth cultivating, Seth." He poured the old rancher a cup of coffee. "What're you doin' in town?"

"Huntin' for work." Seth frowned, sipping his coffee, then looked at it. "Damn, that's terrible stuff. Give you the thumps." He looked at the sheriff. "You hear of anything?"

Quade shook his head grimly. "Sorry, Seth, I haven't. Rough summer for everybody."

"Yeah." The old rancher frowned.

"Who's that you brought in?" Milt Chambers asked.

Seth glanced back over his shoulder. "Some fella had car trouble. Headed for Grass River."

Quade's mouth widened in amused disbelief. "You're pullin' it."

"No." Seth shook his head.

"Grass River," Chambers said, looking out the window. "What the hell would anybody want up there?"

"Not my concern," the old rancher sighed, resting back in his chair.

"Say what his name was?" Chambers asked.

"McCord, I think," Seth said. "Dave."

"McCord," Milt repeated the name. "Sounds familiar."

"Mad-dog killer, maybe," the sheriff said, smiling.

The deputy blinked, pained. "Damnit, Tom, I was just wonderin' . . ."

Quade's smile faded and a trace of regret replaced it. "I'm sorry, Milt. You're right. It could be familiar. Tell you what— you take those boys down to court on those drunk charges and we'll talk about it later."

Chambers nodded reluctantly. "Right away," he said, getting to his feet.

"And, Milt . . ."

"Yeah," the deputy replied, hesitating.

"Stop worryin'. You're doin' all right. Just take it easy."

Chambers blinked, his eyes hardening. "Easy don't get it done." He frowned, then nodded sharply. "See you later," he said and left.

Watching him, Quade shook his head and looked back to Seth. "Was I all that fired up when you broke me in, Seth?"

The old man grinned vaguely. "Not quite."

Quade leaned back in his chair. "You could always go on part time for me. You're still the best shot I know of."

Seth shook his head. "You'd be doin' it just as a favor, Tom. I'd rather not get my money like that. 'Sides, I gave up hunting men a long time ago."

Quade finished his coffee and pushed away his cup. "You been to the bank?"

Seth scowled. "What's that old sayin'? 'Gotta prove you don't need it 'fore you can get it'—somethin' like that. My dad started that place on his word. Walked in and told 'em he needed money to get goin', and they gave it to him." He sighed wearily. "Man's word don't mean much anymore."

"Those days are gone," Quade said.

"The days," the old man nodded, "and the men." He forced a smile on his face. "'Cept you and me, and I'm seventy years old." Pushing his chair away from the table, he stood up. "Got things to do," he said. "You hear of anything, let me know."

"Will do," the sheriff said and watched him leave. His eyes stayed with the old man as he got into his truck and drove away. He felt a deep frown pulling through his mouth. "Damn . . ." he whispered. "Damn . . ."

Dave McCord pushed through the door of the hotel and, slipping his pack off, leaned against the counter and rang the bell. Muffled voices came from beyond the door and behind the counter and a moment later it opened a crack, and a balding man peered out questioningly.

"What can I do for you?"

"Mr. Edwards?"

"Yeah."

"I'd like a room."

"A room?"

Dave pushed his hat back. "You do rent rooms, don't you?"

"Sure thing." The man nodded. "Wait a second," he said, grinning, "gotta get my pants on." The door closed for a minute, then the balding man rushed out, buckling his belt and smoothing down the colorless memory of hair on his head. "Gotta pardon me," he grinned again, "don't get many people this time of year."

Dave shook his head. "That's all right."

Edwards handed him a key. "Number ten," he said, and turned the register for McCord to sign.

Dave stared at the book for a moment, then wrote the name David Martin, and slipped the key into his pocket. "Thanks," he said, nodded, then looked up at the hotel man. "Fella named Mattick said I might buy some horses from you."

"Horses?" His grin widened. "Sure thing. What'd you need?"

"A saddle horse and a pack animal."

"Sure thing," Edwards replied.

"When can I look at 'em?"

"Now, if you like. They're all right down behind the hotel. Got my barn and corral down there. Run trips in the summer. Real good rates."

"Can I leave this stuff here?" Dave pointed at his pack and the rifle.

Edwards nodded. "All winter. Town this size can't support many thieves."

"All right." Dave smiled, then followed as Edwards led him down a hall through the hotel to the back. Down a hill were a barn and corral. The mountains rose behind them.

"You know," Edwards offered as they went into the barn, "if you're just goin' campin', I can rent all this stuff to you."

Dave shook his head. "No. I'll be needing them awhile." Starting down the barn, he looked over the horses. "All of 'em for sale?"

"'Cept the bay," Edwards pointed out, "and the black."

Dave nodded and walked the length of the barn, then came back up to a stall containing a sorrel. Going into the stall, he ran his hand over the animal's back, then checked his hooves, flanks, belly, and mouth.

"I'll take him," he said, coming out of the stall.

Edwards grinned. "You know your horses."

"Which one would you recommend for a pack animal?"

The balding man peered back up through the barn, considering. "The brown," he finally said, gesturing to a big animal at the other end of the barn.

"Good enough," Dave agreed. "How about gear?"

"Got plenty. Canned goods too, if you need 'em. Jerky, coffee, pilot bread, and such. Bought it for them pack trips and didn't use it all. 'Course, for your bulk stuff you'll have to go to the store."

"Fine," Dave said. "Put the equipment out here next to the stalls. I'll leave it to you."

Edwards nodded.

"Another thing," Dave added, "I'll need somebody with a horse trailer to take me and these horses up to Grass River. Can you do that, too?"

Edwards blinked. "Sure thing, but, son, you know Grass River's a—"

"I know," Dave grinned, "a ghost town. Can you take me up there?"

"Sure." Edwards nodded slowly. "But ain't you got a car?"

"Had some trouble with it," Dave explained, then smiled. "If you'll figure what I owe you, I'll pay you later. I'd like to leave about six in the morning if that's all right with you."

"Sure thing." Edwards shrugged, a little bewildered. "Listen, though, if it's just camping you want, south of here's best. I take folks down there all the time. 'Round the lakes and all."

Dave shook his head. "No," he said, and his eyes drifted to the peaks. "How 'bout up in there?"

Edwards followed his gaze. "The Leyendas? Not hardly. Only folks I know go in there are an old sheepherder, Asa Rule and his daughter, Annie. Nothin' but rough country up in there. So damn bad they can't even get a road through it. You were askin' about Grass River . . ."

"Yeah."

Edwards pointed as he said, "Well, it's northwest of here across the Leyendas a hundred or so miles, but the road there is off that way," he swung his arm west, "hundred and fifty miles. Have to go around. Yeah," he nodded, "damn rough country. What city folks'd call a wilderness area." He looked at Dave. "You ain't thinkin' of goin' in there, too?"

"No," Dave said, "just up to Grass River and the Wild Horse Range."

"Hell," Edwards grumbled, "they're worse than these."

Dave's eyes softened. "I know." He nodded, then looked back

up toward the hotel. "Think I'll find that bed," he sighed. "Thanks for your help, Mr. Edwards."

In his room, Dave walked to the window overlooking the highway. Seth's old truck was gone from in front of the restaurant.

So was the police car.

Sighing his relief, McCord walked back to his bed and sat down, frowning. He shouldn't have slipped and given the old man his real name.

"Not very good at running," he said aloud. Then, leaning back on his bed, he smiled wearily. It didn't make any difference anyway. The old man wouldn't have any reason to remember his name or tell it to anybody.

Stretching out on the bed, Dave took off his hat and threw it toward a chair. He missed. He meant to get undressed, but eased back onto the blankets instead, thinking to rest a minute, and was instantly asleep.

TWO

Restless, Deputy Milt Chambers checked his watch again.

Twelve-fifteen.

"Damn." He breathed tightly and tried for a countless time to get comfortable on the hardwood court bench. The judge droned on at the drunk in front of him. Milt's eyes moved to the waiting bench on the far wall. Five more to go. The judge went on. He was a reformed drunk himself and loved to give speeches on the evils of alcohol and the beauty of the reformed life. They made Chambers' butt ache.

McCord, the deputy thought. McCord.

He knew he had read or seen that name someplace. He knew he was right. And he was going to prove it to Quade. This wasn't going to be like the last job. . . .

The judge's voice ground into him and he shifted his bony weight on the bench, trying to conform himself to it. Sighing, he glanced at his watch again.

Dave McCord slept until nearly one. Rising and undressing, he stumbled across the room into the bathroom and stepped under the shower. He enjoyed the luxury of the hot water for a long time, then, stepping out and turning off the water, he scrubbed himself dry with a rough hotel towel. He dressed and went downstairs. The lobby and desk were empty as he pushed through the front door.

The cold air outside jerked awareness through him. He ran down the steps, crossed the highway at a half run, and hurriedly entered the grocery store.

There were two people inside. A young woman wearing work-clothes and a man with straw-colored hair bent over, pulling a hundred-pound sack of potatoes. More sacks were stacked near the door. The straw-haired man pulled the potatoes over with the rest, then straightened up, getting his breath.

"Damn, Annie," he wheezed, smiling at the girl, "always get my exercise when you and your dad go up to Foggy Peak." He looked to Dave. "Somethin' I can do for you?"

Dave nodded. "Supplies," he said, taking a list from his pocket and handing it to the storeman.

Taking it, the straw-haired man looked it over carefully. "Enough to stay the winter," he commented.

"That's right," Dave said.

The storeman folded the list and stuffed it into his pocket.

"Be late this afternoon or tonight. Got an order for Annie here."

"Fine." Dave shrugged. "Be back later." He started for the door.

"Right," the clerk nodded. He turned to the girl. "Goin' kind of a sudden, ain't you?"

"Snow," the girl named Ann answered. "Dad thought we had more time. Another month at least, but the snow came early. Fouls the hell out of everything."

At the door, Dave looked back at the girl. The profanity seemed a contradiction to her, yet natural at the same time. She looked a year or two younger than Dave. Light brown hair pushing down from beneath an old hat. Slim under her jeans and heavy coat. An odd, homely beauty rustling in her.

Realizing suddenly that he was staring at her, Dave cleared his throat. "Later on, then," he said, nodded, and hurriedly closed the door behind him.

He crossed the highway and went back into the hotel and rang the bell on the counter. Edwards peered out from behind the door and, seeing Dave, came out.

"Got it all ready for you, son." He smiled.

"Good." Dave nodded. "You have the papers on the horses?"

"Right here," Edwards replied, pulling them out of his shirt pocket. "All notarized."

Dave looked them over and signed them. "How much do I owe you in all?"

Edwards sighed, figuring. "Call it four hundred and fifty."

Dave took out his wallet and counted the bills, then, taking his copy of the papers, folded it and slipped it into the wallet.

Edwards swallowed as he picked up the money. "Good doin' business with you, son."

"The saddle and all out back?"

Edwards folded the bills. "Saddle's on the stall by your sorrel. Pack frame's with the brown, and so's the food."

"Good." Dave nodded and, turning, started down the hall toward the rear door. "See you in the mornin'," he said.

Clouds covered the sky, breathing a false twilight as he ambled down the yard to the barn. Going inside, he found a light switch on the wall and flipped it on. His sorrel and the brown had been moved next to each other near the door at the far end. He checked the saddle and pack frame, then looked into the feed sack of groceries. Those in the sack he would use on the trail, the rest he could secure for later.

Turning, he walked down to the end of the barn and looked north to the peaks drifting in the mist and clouds. Fragments of yesterday left behind.

"Almost to the trees, Heck," he whispered.

Deputy Milt Chambers locked the last of the sentenced drunks in his cell, hung the keys at the main door, then walked back into the office, looking at his watch.

One-twenty.

"Late," he said, frowning.

"Say somethin', son?"

Chambers' eyes came up. The dispatcher, Alf Corey, was peering at him from behind his desk and his radio, age wrinkles gathering his face as he smiled. He smiled at damn near everything.

"Corey," Chambers asked, "you seen those APB's and the other stuff that's come over the wire?"

"Filed," Corey grinned. "Most recent stuff in the drawers under dates."

"Thanks." Chambers nodded and crossed the room to the files.

"Got a line on something?" Corey craned his neck, watching.

Chambers pulled a stack of files from the drawer and placed them on his desk. "Don't know."

Corey shook his head, smiling. "No need goin' at it that hard. Old Tom ain't no ass biter, you know."

"I know," Chambers nodded. "Just want to check somethin' out."

"Work too hard," Corey muttered, shrugging. "Fella you deputied for before musta been some ass biter."

Chambers' eyes jerked up. "Who said I'd deputied before?" he snapped.

Corey swallowed. "Just figgered you had. Other'n filin'—things that's different in most offices—you seem to know your way around pretty good. Procedures and all that."

The deputy tried to shrug his tension away. "Just like the work," he offered, and sat down at his desk.

"What did you do?" Corey asked.

"What?"

"What sorta work did you do?"

"Lot of things," Chambers said, and turned his back on the old man.

Corey shook his head wearily. "What's got you so riled, anyhow? You go at ever'thin' hard. Like you got somethin' to prove."

The deputy turned slightly. "Maybe I have, Corey." He nodded. "Like a fella once told me—'Easy don't get it done,' and I'm gonna prove to him—"

"Who's that?"

Chambers blinked and turned back to the papers on his desk. "Nobody," he answered. "I've got work to do, Corey, now let me get to it."

The dispatcher started to say something else when a call came over the radio. He answered it.

Chambers glanced up at Corey, watching him for a moment, then, frowning, he began going through the papers.

Seth Mattick and George McDonald ambled the distance between McDonald's feeding lot and his house.

McDonald, a friend of twenty-five years, was shaking his head. "I'd like to, Seth, you know that, but the truth is, I'm havin' to let a couple of boys go. Summer was pretty bad. Wish I could say I'd loan it to you, but I can't even do that."

Seth nodded. "Wouldn't want it that way, Mac." They came to Seth's pickup and stopped. "Well, hope you make it through," Seth said.

McDonald shrugged. "I'll make it. Hope you do, too," he said and, slapping Seth on the shoulder, started back toward the lot. "Gotta get some work done." He frowned. "See you, Seth."

Watching him, the old rancher felt a trembling twist in his stomach. He had never felt so damn helpless in his whole life. He had to do something. Anything. And there was nothing he could do.

"Damn," he growled angrily, and climbed into his old pickup.

He was bouncing down the road, headed for his place, when he saw the first flakes fall. His hands tightened on the wheel and he looked up. The clouds had moved down from the peaks. Blending white and blue-black, the flakes materializing suddenly. Latticing away the sun, falling with deadly beauty.

"Damn," he said, frowning as he pushed back in the seat. "Looks like you're up against it now, old man."

In his room, Dave McCord saw the snow come. Crossing to the window, he watched it for a long time. Funny how you could love and hate something at the same time. The falling snow gave him an almost sensuous murmur, yet he knew getting into the high country of Wild Horse Range would be harder now. Remembering the girl back in the store, he smiled. She was right. It did foul the hell out of everything.

He turned away from the window and, taking his coat off the bed, pulled it on and went downstairs.

Edwards sat in an overstuffed chair beneath a dim light, squinting at a newspaper. He looked up as Dave came down the stairs.

"Know a good place to eat?" he asked the hotel owner.

"Pride's, I suppose," Edwards grinned. "Ain't much of a choice this time of the year." He nodded at the window. "Snow's gonna make it a little rough on you, ain't it?"

"A little," Dave agreed and, turning, ambled outside into the snow. He looked up through the colorless kaleidoscope and smiled.

The snow didn't matter. A little trouble didn't matter. He was going to make it after all. And that's all that mattered.

Deputy Milt Chambers eased back in his chair, a frown pressing through his lips.

"Damn," he grumbled wearily and shook his head.

"Somethin' wrong?" Corey asked from the radio.

"Been two weeks back in these files and there's not a damn thing here," he said impatiently, sighing.

"May be further back than that."

Chambers shook his head. "No," he said, "it hasn't even been a week that I saw that name. Did two weeks to be sure."

Corey shrugged and sat back in the chair. "Maybe it wasn't a felony."

Chambers looked around. "What?"

"Maybe it wasn't a felony," Corey repeated, and pointed at the stack of files on the desk. "You got the felony wires there."

Chambers looked at the files again. "I thought you said you filed them by date."

"I do," Corey nodded. "Ever'thin's filed by date, the felonies in one file, ever'thin' else in the other file there. Told you about that a couple of weeks ago," the radio man explained, watching as the deputy jumped out of the chair and rushed to the files. "Tom likes to be able to find the serious stuff right off. . . ."

Standing at the files, Chambers only half listened as he rustled through the papers. Yesterday. The day before. Three days ago.

Hurrying, he almost went by it, then jerked the sheet of paper from the file.

MCCORD, DAVID, WMA, 6′2″ 180 BRN GRN MISSING HOOVER PRIVATE HOSPITAL POSSIBLY DRIVING 1973 CORV BLU COLO XA 422 REWARD 3000 DENVER SHERIFF

"Find it?" Corey asked.

Chambers nodded. "Mental patient, it looks like," he answered. "Where's Tom?"

"Out at Schaffer's. You want me to call him to see what to do?"

"No." Chambers shook his head. "I can take care of it." Crossing to his desk, he picked up the telephone and dialed Bob Sims's number.

"Three Medicine Wrecking Service. Bob here."

"Bob, Milt Chambers. You bring in a blue Corvette for a fella named McCord this morning?"

"Corvette? McCord? No, sure haven't, Milt. What's the problem?"

"Talkin' to Seth this mornin'. Gave a fella a ride into town. He had car trouble—figured you might have pulled it in."

"Yeah. Fella named Martin. Green Ford."

Milt shook his head. "No, Bob, one I need is named McCord. Driving a Corvette."

"No, sorry, Milt."

"Listen, Bob, check, will you?"

"No need. That Martin fella is the only business I've had today. Called from Seth's. You know, he's gonna junk the damn thing."

Chambers' shoulders slumped. "Okay, Bob, thanks anyway."

"Sure, Milt. Anytime."

The deputy replaced the receiver and looked at the APB again.

"Wrong fella?" Corey asked.

"Bob Sims says his name is Martin, but this morning Seth Mattick said his name was McCord."

"Martin—McCord, they sound alike. Seth coulda made a mistake."

Chambers shook his head. "Not from what I've heard about that old man."

Corey smiled. "That's true enough."

Chambers stood. "Well, there's one thing I can do."

"What's that?"

"Have a look at his driver's license. Be impossible for him to get a new one in three days."

In the Pride Restaurant Dave McCord was raising a piece of steak to his mouth when he saw the police car pull up in front of the hotel. He watched through the foggy window as the car door opened and a man rushed inside.

McCord's stomach tightened as he slipped the meat into his mouth and chewed slowly, his eyes staying on the hotel.

The man came back out of the hotel past the car into the street.

Dave set his fork down, stiffening. He looked to the street door, then to the one leading out the side.

The man was in the middle of the street now. Dave could make out his uniform coat.

Fighting the panic exploding in him, he made himself stay where he was. He couldn't make it out now without paying his check and drawing attention to himself.

The uniformed man came up on the walk and into the restaurant. He glanced over the room and, seeing Dave, came toward him.

"David Martin?" he asked.

Dave looked up, sipping his coffee. "That's right."

"Wonder if I could see your driver's license?"

Dave glanced around the room, then smiled. "Was I going too fast?"

The deputy's mouth hardened. "Just let me see it."

Dave moved his shoulders apologetically. "Afraid I don't have it with me."

"Why's that?"

"Took it out and left it in my pack. Along with some other things. Credit cards and the like."

"Can I ask why?"

Dave smiled. "Because the last time I went hunting I stepped into a creek and ruined it all. Had to get it all new."

The deputy nodded. "Could we go over and get it?"

"Sure." Dave shrugged. "What's the trouble?"

"Have an APB out for a man with your description."

Dave grinned. "My description? You're kidding."

"No," the deputy said. "Now if we could just have a look at that driver's license I'll leave you alone."

"Sure." Dave shrugged again. Fighting to stay calm, he got to his feet and walked to the cashier. He paid his ticket, then he and the deputy ducked into the snow.

They rushed across the highway through the snow and into the hotel. The lobby and desk were empty as the two men turned up the stairs.

Climbing, Dave shook his head, smiling. "Fella really looks like me you say?"

"Yeah," the deputy nodded.

"That's enough to get him arrested right there," Dave said, forcing himself to make conversation.

The deputy smiled slightly.

"Gotta check ever'thin' out," he explained, and Dave felt the edge leave his voice. The deputy had relaxed a little now and that's what he needed.

They came up into the hall and Dave fished his key from his pocket, tugging it free from the material.

"Always put the number on the biggest piece of plastic they can find," Dave grumbled, finally getting it out and putting it in the lock.

"Yeah," the deputy agreed.

Dave opened the door, leaving the key in the lock. He stepped into the room. The deputy followed.

His pack and rifle stood leaning against the wall next to the bathroom door. Dave felt his breath thicken and his heart jerk as he looked to the deputy and made himself smile easily.

"Don't know what procedure is in this sort of thing, but I really don't want to move toward that rifle while you think I might be wanted. You mind getting the pack and I'll get my stuff out of it?"

The deputy sighed heavily. "Look, Mr. Martin, I—" Frowning, he shook his head. "Might as well go ahead and look while I'm up here." He turned toward the pack and rifle.

His back was toward Dave.

And Dave stepped into him, thrusting both his hands into the deputy's back, shoving him forward into the bathroom, stumbling into the tub.

"Hey!" he yelled.

Dave slammed the bathroom door, grabbed his pack and rifle, and was charging through the door when he heard the bathroom door tearing open. Pulling the hall door to, Dave twisted the key in the lock, jerked it out, and ran.

"McCord!" the deputy barked. "Goddamnit, McCord—"

Plummeting down the stairs, the crack of wood followed Dave. He turned at the bottom of the stairs and, running as hard as he could, burst down the hall and through the back door.

In the room, Milt Chambers slammed his shoulder into the door again. The heavy oak held. Standing back, he kicked the lock, driving his booted foot into it twice.

It held.

Glancing frantically about the room, he bolted to the window and, ramming it up and open, looked out. It was a clear drop to the ground.

Reeling, he looked at the door again. His hand brushed his pistol and he glanced down.

"Jesus," he barked. Reaching into his coat, drew the pistol, cocked it, and crossed to the door. The first shot smashed the lock. The second blew it away. Kicking the door open, the deputy crashed into the hall, then down the stairs.

Bill Edwards was stepping from behind the desk as the deputy came to the bottom of the stairs.

"What the hell is goin' on?" he demanded in a trembling voice as Chambers rushed by him and out the front door. Standing on the front porch of the hotel, Chambers looked up and down the street.

Nothing moved. Only the snow.

Pivoting, he charged back inside, nearly running into Edwards.

"That shootin'—" the hotel man stuttered.

"That fella, Martin. You seen him?"

"No. Did he—"

"He didn't come this way?"

"No." Edwards shook his head. "He might be down at the barn."

"The barn? What the hell for?"

"Bought a horse. He—"

"A horse?" the deputy growled, and was running, leaving Edwards mumbling to himself.

At the sound of the shots, Dave McCord was throwing the saddle on his newly bought sorrel. The sharp, muffled thumps jerked his eyes up and around.

Turning back to the horse, he moved deftly and quickly. Cinching and tightening. Pulling the bridle on. Leading the horse out of the stall and snatching up the food sack and pack on the ground, hooking them on the saddle horn. With the rifle in his hand, he swung up into the saddle, running the horse up the aisle and through the doors into the snow, pulling his head around, shouting him north toward the mountains.

Running.

Behind him, Milt Chambers crashed through the door in time to see a slight movement of color in the blending white.

"McCord!" he screamed and, raising his pistol, he fired once, then again.

And the man on the horse was gone, running in the white, pulling up the pasture into the hills and the mountains beyond.

THREE

Seth Mattick had made a fresh pot of coffee and, pouring himself a cup, he went outside in his shirt-sleeves and stood on the porch. Ignoring the cold, he swept his eyes over the yard, the hopelessness from the afternoon stronger now.

Frowning, he turned to go inside when he saw the flicker of car lights through the pine and cottonwoods along the road. The lights dipped out of sight, then brushed over the house as a car pushed up the hill and parked by the porch.

Seth smiled. It was Tom Quade.

"What're you doin' out this way, Sheriff?" the old man called as Quade climbed out of the car and started around.

"Got a problem, Seth," he said, coming up the steps.

The tone in Quade's voice brushed the smile from Seth's mouth. "Come on in," he said, and they went inside to the kitchen. Taking off his hat, Quade sat down at the table.

"Coffee?" Seth offered.

"Yeah."

Seth poured another cup and put it down beside Quade.

"Serious?" the old man asked.

Quade smiled wearily. "Ain't it always? That fella you brought into town—"

"Young fella this mornin'?"

"The same." Quade nodded. "Turns out that there's a want on him. Walked out of a rest home three days ago. Milt tried to bring him in, and he escaped. Went north on horseback."

Seth put down his cup. "North? You mean up into the mountains?"

Quade nodded.

"Jesus." Seth sighed amazedly. "What the hell's he gonna do in there?"

Quade shrugged. "Beats the hell out of me. Like I said, he walked out of a rest home."

"A mental patient?"

"Looks that way."

The old man thought for a moment, then shook his head. "It don't sit right."

"What's that?"

"Him bein' crazy. I talked to him. Spent time with him." He shook his head again. "That boy's no more crazy than I am."

Quade smiled. "Wondered when you would admit it."

Seth smiled, too, and, getting to his feet, he brought the coffee-pot to the table, pouring out two more cups.

"You think he's dangerous?" Seth asked.

"Don't know." The sheriff shrugged. "He broke arrest."

"He still have the rifle?"

Quade nodded heavily.

The old rancher sipped his coffee. "Got any idea what it's all about?"

"Not much," Quade replied, grimacing as he eased back in his chair. "Some kind of fight in the rest home. A breakdown they say. Put him in the rest home. Deputy I talked to didn't know much about it, and the file didn't say much."

The two men sat quietly for a moment, then Seth pushed away his cup. "You're out here to get me to go in with you, I take it."

"Pretty much," Tom nodded.

Seth's face shadowed. "I gave all that up twenty years ago."

Tom frowned. "I know."

"I've got too much to do here, Tom. Hell, me and this place are about to go under.

"That's another reason I came, Seth."

The old man looked up. "What?"

A frown deepened on the sheriff's mouth. "I didn't want to

say it quite this way—but—there's a three-thousand-dollar reward for him."

"Three thousand? Who the hell? He's not a felon. Who'd put up that kind of money?"

"Family," the sheriff explained. "Done a lot these days. There are so many missing persons that the police can't keep up with 'em. Families put up the money to attract private operators. That's what they've done here. Three thousand dollars for information leading to the return of Dave McCord."

"Looks like anybody could collect."

Quade shook his head. "The return part of it keeps it in tow. He's got to be brought back for anybody to collect the money."

Seth stood up from the table. "Bounty money," he whispered heavily. "Never went after anybody for bounty."

"I know that," Quade said quietly.

The old man shook his head. "Hell, I—" he began, then sighed it away. "Let me call you tomorrow morning early. If I decide to go, we can leave then."

Nodding, the sheriff began to turn. He wanted to say something to the old rancher but couldn't think of what it would be. His eyes caught the glint of the rifle above the mantle.

"See you still have the Henry."

The old man looked around, a wan smile trying to push through his lips. "You've coveted that damn thing ever since I can remember."

"No chance of your givin' it to me?"

Seth's smile was dark. "The day I miss with it."

The sheriff reflected the smile understandingly. "Ever find out what it's worth? Quite a bit, a gun that old, and in good shape."

"Don't know," Seth said. "Never thought about sellin' it."

Tom nodded. "Seth," he began with difficulty, "there's no shame—"

"I'll call you tomorrow mornin' one way or another," the old rancher cut him off. "I just want to think about it."

"Yeah." The sheriff frowned and almost hurried out the door.

Seth watched the car pull out, then slip away in the darkness and snow. Pouring himself another cup of coffee, his eyes moved back to the Henry and the pictures beneath it.

His sons, Harve and Ernie, in the summer of 1941. Harve, eighteen. Ernie, seventeen.

And his wife, Ella. Nineteen years old in that picture taken nearly forty years ago. Her father's house and a sheepdog in the background.

He could remember that she had grayed, and her face had lined, but that was blurred, only an echoing murmur of pain and loss. Now, she was always nineteen years old for him.

"Wish you were here," he said quietly. "'Specially at times like this. We're gonna lose it, Ella. Hell," he sighed, "it ain't even for you anymore, is it? Or the boys. Harve doesn't want it, and Ernie's dead. Just me tryin' to hold on."

Turning off the light, he eased down in an old chair, staring out the window. He couldn't see Ella's picture anymore, but he could feel her there, like he could always feel her in the house. As if what she'd touched rustled with her memory. He had taken out the wall between the kitchen and living room so that it would be all one. So that whoever was in their house wouldn't be separated. People. People were important to her. That was why he'd promised to give up his job as sheriff.

Twenty years ago he'd finally had to kill a man, and later, looking at Ella's face, he knew she could never live with him if he had to kill again. And more important, he knew he couldn't live with himself.

So he'd given it up and never regretted it.

He looked back in the direction of the pictures. Now he was going to lose the ranch, unless he went out one more time.

Once more.

It was the hint of bounty that made it distasteful to him. There was really nothing wrong with it, he told himself.

Except he didn't like hunting a man for money.

His stomach twisted and he nodded. He had to do something. And this was his only out.

"Ella," he said aloud, whispering her name. "Gotta do some-thin'," he murmured. "I have to."

A rustle of sunlight in the snow, blurred and wandering white, woke him in his chair. Blinking, then jerking up, he looked at the clock on the mantle. Five-thirty. Morning stirred in the pictures and was gray in the yellow metal of the Henry. Ghosts like memories of voices. Breathing yesterday. Watching.

"Damn," he growled, turning away, walking into the kitchen. He dialed Tom Quade's number.

A sleepy voice mumbled, "Quade, what is it?"

"You still in bed?"

"Seth?"

"Goin' soft, Tom. That belly is gettin' to you. If we're goin' let's go."

The line was silent.

"Tom?"

"I heard you," the sheriff said. "I'll be there in an hour."

"I'll have a horse for you," he said and hung up.

Tom Quade rested the receiver back into the cradle and looked back across the bed to his wife, Norma. She was sitting up, pushing her brown hair from sleepy eyes.

"Coffee and . . . ?" she asked.

Quade glanced at his stomach, then, frowning, said, "Eggs, sausage, pancakes. Maybe I'll ride it off."

Nodding, she pulled herself out of bed and went into the kitchen. He dressed quickly and warmly, then went in to break-fast. She poured him a third cup of coffee when he was finished, but he shook his head.

"Need to go to work," he said.

"Take care," she said, and he could see more in her eyes. It was always there, but she never said it. She didn't have to.

"I will," he whispered and, leaning down, hugged her tightly, then left hurriedly.

He drove down the highway to his office. The dispatcher,

Corey, was at the radio and Milt Chambers was drinking coffee at his desk. He looked up as Tom came in, and then down again.

Frowning, Quade shook his head. "Milt," he said, "you still broodin' about that fella gettin' away?"

"A little." The young deputy shrugged.

"Well, stop," the sheriff ordered him. "You made some mistakes. You'll learn."

"Yeah," the deputy sighed. He looked up. "Seth call?"

"He did," the sheriff said.

"We goin' in?"

"Me and Seth are."

"Aw, Tom," Chambers complained, "it was me that lost him. Let—"

"Look," Quade snapped, "you want me to treat you like a man, act like a professional instead of a damn kid playin' a game. That's what got you into this." He shook his head, sighing sympathetically. "Milt," he said, the edge out of his voice, "you go at it too hard. Ease up."

"Sure." Chambers nodded.

"Get me a rifle, will you, and some shells, then drive me out to Seth's."

"Right," the deputy replied, nodding.

Quade watched him for a moment, then, frowning, he turned to his desk to write out the procedures while he was gone.

From the phone the old man had gone to the stove and started his coffee, then, pulling two thermoses from under the sink, he placed them on the counter next to the stove. While the coffee was cooking he began putting together a food sack. The coffee finished and he poured part of it into one of the thermoses, the rest into a cup for himself, then started a new pot. Going into the bedroom, he shed his clothes and put on his thermal underwear, then dressed again.

From the closet he took a heavy wool shirt, another pair of pants, wool socks, and his bedroll, then took them into the kitchen. Placing the bedroll on the table, Seth looked it over. Made of a tarpaulin, white ducking, and two heavy quilts between, it was the best bed a man could have on the trail. On well-drained ground, he would be dry, and in the snow, the weight of the snow would help keep him warm. It wasn't quite as fancy or light as the new sleeping bags, but it did the job and then some. He'd made it himself thirty years ago and only had to make minor repairs now and then.

Folding the extra clothes, he put them into the roll, bound it up, then placed it by the door.

He made breakfast, ate, and was finishing pouring coffee into the thermos when he heard the car pull up outside. Taking three cups from the shelves, he filled them and put them on the table. Tom Quade and Milt Chambers burst through the door without knocking.

"Jesus," the deputy shivered. "I don't envy you two."

"Just don't let it run you," Seth said.

"What?" Milt looked up.

"Cold," Seth said. "Less you think about it, less it bothers you, that's all. Can't let things like cold run you." He pointed at the table. "Coffee," he said.

Milt shook his head puzzledly' and Quade smiled, picking up a cup.

The old rancher looked to the sheriff. "What do you think, Tom?"

The sheriff shrugged. "He may have gone further in. He may have circled back to the highway."

Seth shook his head. "I don't think so," he said. "Somethin' he said to me yesterday sticks in my mind. Got your map?"

Reaching into his coat, the sheriff pulled out a folded mass of paper and, pushing the coffee cups aside, spread it on the table.

"Here's what he went into last night," Seth said, pointing to a large oblong shape on the map. The area was bordered by what were marked as farm roads. Within the roads it was blank except for elevation points and a chain of inverted v's denoting the Leyenda Mountain Range running northeast to south central, ending just above Three Medicine.

"A hundred and twenty miles this way"—Seth gestured north and south—"two hundred and four that way"—he swept his hand east and west—"and not a goddamn thing out there but hard times." He looked at the sheriff. "Remember I talked to him yesterday? Asked where he was headed. Northwest of Three Medicine, across the Leyendas." He put his finger on the northern edge of the wilderness area. "Grass River."

Milt Chambers looked up incredulously. "Grass River? You mean he's headed all the way across that rattlesnake farm?"

"That's what I'm sayin'." The old man nodded.

The sheriff joined him. "I think you're right," he said. "Edwards at the hotel said McCord was dead set on goin' up there. Into the Wild Horse Range for the winter." Quade nodded again. "Yeah, Seth, I think you hit it."

"Jesus," the deputy sighed, "all the way across the Leyendas. He is crazy."

"Not really," the old man said. "Not when you look at it. The Wild Horse Range comes right down to Grass River. He can't get there by road—police'd have it covered. His only way is across here. Even in good weather planes'd have a helluva time spottin' him, and right now one can't even get off the ground. He's got that goin' for him."

"Yeah." Tom frowned.

"But we've got a couple of things goin' for us," Seth pointed out. "Grass River is northwest of here. The mountains above town head off northeast. If he took the eastern slope of the mountains, he's gonna run into Asa Rule pushin' his sheep up to the sheltered pasture at Foggy Peak. If he is on the eastern slope, the first place to cross the mountains toward Grass River is just below Foggy—"

"You figger he's on the eastern slope," Tom said.

"Natural way out of Three Medicine."

"Ain't this a road leadin' part way to Asa's?" The deputy pointed at the map. "Shows one here. Go in that way."

Seth smiled sourly. "State likes to claim any excuse for a road. Callin' it a trail is bein' kind. Nothin' but a cut in the timber." He nodded. "I thought about it. Be easier, but it depends on him goin' up the eastern slope. If he went the other way and I'm guessin' wrong, we'd lose him."

The old man shook his head. "No, somebody's got to follow him up. But what you said ain't a bad idea. Have somebody try and get to Asa's by way of that track. Maybe cut him off. At any rate, if we catch up with him it'll be a lot shorter goin' out that way than ridin' all the way back."

The deputy looked to Quade hopefully, but kept his voice calm. "You . . . want me to ride up that way, Tom?"

Quade considered it for a moment, then nodded. "Sounds like a good idea."

"Okay." Milt grinned. "I'll be there tomorrow."

Seth smiled patiently. "You ever been up in the Leyendas?"

"No, sir."

"Takes a little time to get around up in there. We'll get to Asa's day after tomorrow. If you start tomorrow—even using that so-called road—you'll get there about the same time. That is if you can get there at all."

"I can do it." The deputy nodded. "Two days, then."

"And bring a walkie-talkie with you," Quade said.

"Right."

Quade nodded wearily. "My stuff is out in the car. Take it down to the barn, will you?"

"Sure." Milt smiled and went back out to the car.

Quade looked to Seth.

"Ready?" he asked.

Seth picked up his bedroll and the food sack, and his eyes went to the Henry over the mantle.

"Been a long time," he said quietly.

Quade swallowed. "Likely you won't even use it."

Seth glanced at him. "Yeah." He nodded and, crossing the room, took it down from the wall and turned to Quade.

"Let's go," he said.

Five minutes later the two men were on horseback, pushing up the hills, riding. And the movement of the horse kindled an ache in Seth. Not of Ella, but of hunting, and great drifts of mountains like seas, waiting.

FOUR

Dave McCord finished his cup of bitter instant coffee and glanced up into the snowfall shadowing the pines.

No planes today. He nodded and turned to check the can of stew cooking on the single flame butane stove, then looked at his watch again.

Nine o'clock. He frowned.

"We've slept too long," he said to his sorrel.

The sorrel stared at him blankly and, nodding, Dave shrugged. "All right, *I* did." He smiled and, leaving the can on the burner, rolled up his sleeping bag, then transferred equipment from the backpack to the food sack and saddlebags.

Setting aside the empty pack, he took off the can of stew and replaced it with a small pan full of snow. He ate the stew hungrily, then used his bare finger to get at the last of it.

He used the melted-snow water to make another cup of instant coffee. Sipping it, he looked west to the blur of mountains.

The sorrel shifted his feet restlessly and Dave looked back at him, then smiled, nodding.

"You're right," he admitted, "we're wastin' time."

He drained the cup, then gathered his gear together, saddled the horse, and tied on the food sack and saddlebags. Turning from the horse, he slipped his hunting knife from beneath his coat, knelt down, and scooped out a hole. Into it he threw his backpack and the empty tin, then covered them over.

He looked over the campsite a last time, then mounted the sorrel. He took a compass from his coat pocket, checked it for direction, then, slipping it back in his coat, he turned the sorrel into the trees.

The snow ebbed through the scrawls of pine, aspen, and birch, whispering pale, dumb memories of themselves in a theft of giving.

An odd heaviness webbed Dave's stomach, stretching through him. Anonymous shapes shifted and suddenly he felt like an intruder. Pushing up a long rise, he came out of the trees on a crest and, blinking, stopped.

The land rushed away from him, lifting to the peaks on one side, drifting into a white darkness of hills and mesas and canyons to the east, bound in an echo of distance.

The heaviness in Dave's stomach rustled, becoming a part of the distance, and suddenly he didn't know whether he was frightened or overjoyed. Or both.

For a moment he looked back the way he'd come, then, turning front in the saddle, he eased the sorrel over the rise.

Seth and Tom Quade moved up the hills, Seth in the lead, leaning out of the saddle, his eyes on the ground.

An hour out, he dismounted and examined the snow carefully.

"Someone's been here," he said, nodding. "Goin' up the east side."

Quade looked at the ground. He couldn't see anything. "How the hell can you tell?"

"Little of the tracks left," he said, then smiled as he mounted. "But not much. Not easy to see something when you don't know what you're lookin' for."

"I'll take your word for it."

They pushed out again, threading the hills, Seth's eyes still on the ground. The snow thickened and after another hour the old man drew up and shook his head.

"Lost it," he grumbled, then pointed up the hills, "He's in there," he nodded, "I'd bet on it. If I had any money—" He started to smile, but it darkened. "Guess I will though, won't I?"

"Stop worryin' about it," Tom said.

"Yeah," the old man replied, frowning. "Just that part of it still bothers me."

"You still don't think he's sick?"

"Not really. You get a feelin' about people, Tom."

Riding across a low ridge, Dave McCord saw a tremble of motion in the flat below him. At first he thought he was seeing things, then, smiling, realized that it was a herd of sheep. The snow had thinned and he could see dark bundles of movement in and out of the sheep. It was almost like a ballet watching the dogs work the sheep. Dave's eyes scanned the snow and finally picked out two riders, one at the rear and another off to one side, leading two pack horses.

Nudging his sorrel out, Dave followed the herd, staying on the ridgeline until it drifted into the flat and the snow.

Looking north, and then back down at the herd, he shrugged and pushed his horse on down toward the rolling mass of wool. Nearing them, he could hear the dogs barking and the rattle of bells.

As he approached, the rider at the rear halted his horse, turned, and rode back toward Dave.

The sheepherder was a small, narrow-shouldered man with a weathered face that could have been anywhere between fifty and one hundred years old.

The sheepherder nodded as he closed the distance between them.

"Asa Rule," he called.

"Dave McCord."

Rule nodded, glancing around. "You know where you are, Dave?"

Dave grinned innocently. "As a matter of fact, I don't, Mr. Rule. I was with a party out of Edwards' down in Three Medicine. Got separated from them last night. Am I headed for town?"

Rule sighed patiently. "You're close to thirty miles north of Three Medicine."

Dave cocked his head. "That right? Jesus, I really am one lost pilgrim." His eyes moved past Rule to the second rider coming up behind him, and he smiled with recognition. It was the girl that had been in the store the afternoon before.

"My daughter, Ann," Rule said.

"Miss," Dave said, nodding, and she smiled in return.

"Yeah, I'd say you were lost, young fella," Rule went on. "Guess I can take you on up to my place and take you out from there. Right now I've got sheep to take care of."

"No chance of me just turning around?"

Rule shrugged. "You can do what you like. 'Course, your chances of gettin' back are about as good as gettin' a suntan out here. Best stay with us."

Dave shrugged. "Guess I'll take up sheepherding for a while."

Nodding, Rule gestured to his daughter. "Got some thermos coffee. Get some in you." He turned his horse out. "Right now, I've got to go to work."

Dave looked at the girl. "Did he say coffee?"

She nodded and, reaching back into a leather sack, pulled out a bottle and poured him a cup of coffee. The smell filtered through the falling snow, putting the taste into his mouth before he had the cup in hand.

Sipping the coffee, he noticed the girl watching him questioningly.

He swallowed a mouthful. "In the store yesterday," he said.

She nodded. "I remember."

Dave finished his coffee and he and the girl caught up with the herd. The air mingled with the sounds of dogs, leather, sheep, and bells.

Dave shook his head and smiled. "I've always known some sheep wear bells, but I never knew why."

Ann restrained a smile. "For marking purposes. As a matter of fact they're called markers. No big bunch of sheep could go far without a marker along. So if we lose some we can always hear them."

"Any other handy information I should know?"

"Just that sheep are stupid—"

A scream ripped the air from behind them.

"Damn," Ann swore, dropping the leads to the pack horses, kicking her own animal out, then wheeling him around to run back in the direction they'd come.

Dave watched her, and the scream came again, a mixture of horror and pain. Pulling the sorrel around, Dave followed the girl. Ahead of him, he could see her pulling a rifle from its boot as she plunged over an embankment down into a creekbed. He heard the sharp report of a shot, and as he went over the embankment he saw Ann stop and lower herself from the saddle.

On the ground was the bloodied mass of wool. Ann raised her rifle, and the sound of the shot jerked through his stomach.

He reined in beside her.

"What happened?" he asked.

The girl looked up at him. "Wolves," she said simply and mounted her horse.

He looked from the dead sheep to the girl. "I'm sorry," he said.

She shook her head. "Nothin' to be sorry for. Nothin' really that can be done about it. Wolf was just doin' what's natural. Killing what's weak." She looked at him. "That's another thing you should know. Out here what's weak, sick, or wounded dies."

As the mountains began to come up on their left, Seth turned toward them.

"Rougher country that way," Quade pointed out.

Seth nodded. "If he has any sense McCord will be on the lower ground. Easier ridin'. When he runs into Asa he'll slow up quite a bit. If we go up through here, we can cut the distance he gained on us."

"You're certain he'll go along with Asa?"

Seth smiled. "Like I said, if he's got any sense. Snow's coverin' his tracks, and he'll figure he's fairly safe. 'Sides, he knows Asa knows the country better than he does. He'll stay with him as long as he can."

"When you figure to be up with him?"

The old man shrugged. "Playin' it safe. Tomorrow mid-mornin'. Maybe noon. I want to make sure we end up even with 'em or ahead of 'em."

Nodding, Quade followed, leading his horse upward. The thinning snow edged back into mist, whispering echoes of mesas and peaks.

The longer Quade rode with Seth, the more amazed he was at the old man. It was almost like Quade wasn't even there. It was just Seth, the horse, and the land they were moving over. More than once Seth halted his horse, then turned slightly, nodded, said, "Snow trap," and was quiet again.

How the hell can he remember every dip in this damn place? the sheriff wondered.

At nightfall Seth led them to a rock overhang and dismounted. Quade glanced up and around. The shelf made a good roof against the snow and wind.

Quade shook his head amazedly. "You ever make a mistake, Seth?"

Dismounting, Seth jerked a look back at the sheriff and grinned suddenly.

"Made too many, Tom. I just remember where I've been."

Leading his horse back against the wall, Seth unsaddled him, ground hitched him, then went to putting down his ground cloth and bedroll.

He looked to Quade.

"You cookin' or am I?"

"You gonna be happy with my coffee?"

"Probably not." Seth nodded. "Get your soggins down and I'll scare up some wood."

Lowering himself to the ground, Quade sighed with relief. He hadn't spent that much time on a horse in ten years. Groaning slightly, he stretched his back, then, squatting and standing, tried to push the mixture of stiffness and numbness out of his knees.

"Jesus," he grumbled.

Carrying an armload of wood, Seth came back to the center of their cover.

"Spend too much time coverin' your butt with your stomach in that car."

"Least it doesn't hurt as bad."

Seth bent down, piling the wood. "Your butt spreads an awful lot though."

Tom glanced over his shoulder.

"Some, I guess." He shrugged. "It's the new look of the law officer. Bright-eyed, fat-bottomed, and pot-bellied."

Seth started the fire.

"You fellas ain't that bad." He stood warming his hands. "Just a little softer."

"Not like the good old days."

Seth looked up at the sheriff, his eyes stark and a little afraid. "No," he said, pulling his eyes away. "Not like the good old days." And brushing by the sheriff, he went to his saddlebags.

Quade watched him for a moment. "What is it, Seth?" he finally asked.

Seth kept his back to him. "What's what?"

Quade frowned, shaking his head. "We've known each other too long, Seth. Somethin' been at you lately. First I thought it was the thing about the ranch, but it's more'n that."

The old rancher brought his saddlebags and the food back to the fire, kneeling down, avoiding Quade's eyes.

"I don't know," he said slowly. "Maybe that's the trouble. I can't quite put my finger on it."

Quade hunched down beside him, taking off his gloves and holding his hands out to the fire.

"What do you mean, Seth?"

"Lotta things, I guess. I'm out here huntin' a fella down to hold on to my place. What's it for?"

"It's your home."

"No." The old man shook his head. "I mean, Ernie's dead, killed in the war. And Harve don't want it. He keeps tellin' me to sell the place and come live in California with him. California, my butt."

"Might be nice," Tom offered.

"Hell, I don't even know him anymore." Seth frowned, and his voice softened as he said, "Ain't his fault. Mine either, I guess. He just changed."

Taking out the coffeepot, Seth filled it with water, then put it on the fire. "No one seems to care about the land anymore. My grandfather and father died here. Just don't seem to be anybody to take their place. Makes you wonder what it was all for. No, it's like you said, the old days are gone, and so are the men." He looked back at the sheriff. "Hell," he sighed, "I get awful mouthy at times. . . ."

He went about his work then, quietly, and without saying anything more to Quade. Quade watched him. They ate in silence.

They were finishing when the howl of a wolf jerked Seth's eyes up.

"What the hell they yowlin' at? Sure as hell can't see the moon."

Seth shook his head. "Little early, but it could be a matin' call."

Quade glanced skeptically at the old man. "Sounds a mite lonesome for a matin' call."

Seth shrugged. "Maybe we sound that lonesome to them when we talk about love." He grinned self-consciously. "Difference is, they don't think about it. That's where they got it over us."

Quade smiled admonishingly. "Damned if you ain't gettin' thoughtful on me, Seth."

A smile pushed at the old man's lips. "Sure sign of age," he said with a wink.

A long way off there was another howl.

Dave McCord looked up at the sound of the wolves, his eyes moving to the door of the large tent they had set up earlier. Inside it, he and Asa sat on folding canvas chairs next to a gasoline heater. Across the tent, Ann was cooking dinner on a gasoline stove.

Asa frowned at the bark of the wolves. "Hungry," he said.

Dave poured himself a cup of coffee from the pot on the heater. "Give you much trouble?"

"Some," Asa allowed. "Quite a bit anymore. Folks put out poison and it kills off the game. It was a dry summer on top of that. Yeah," he sighed, "they'll be hungry this winter."

He looked back to Dave. "Where you from?"

Dave sipped his coffee slowly. "South," he finally answered, "down around Denver. Why do you ask?"

The sheepherder shrugged. "No reason. Spend so much time up here without seein' much of anybody but Annie that when I do, I'm kind of . . . nosy," he said, choosing his words carefully. With a half smile he continued, "Lost all my niceties about the way I poke into their business. What are you doin' in this neck of the woods?"

Dave gazed at him for a moment, then surrendered a smile. "I spent some time up around Grass River with my grandfather. Just wanted to go back and see what it was like. Stopped off at Edwards down in Three Medicine to do a little huntin'. Got myself lost instead."

"That you did," laughed Asa. "'Course, you could take the hard way and keep ridin' after you got to my place," he joked.

Dave forced himself to smile. "How would a fella do that?"

"Go on up to Grass River?" Asa cocked his head. "Take the canyon through the mountains there below my place, I suppose. But if he had any sense he'd turn right around again."

"Why's that?"

"Hard country," the sheepherder explained. "Some of the worst I've ever seen. Wouldn't support a skinny fly." He brought his eyes up. "You say your granddad was from Grass River?"

"Long time ago," Dave said.

"His name McCord, too?"

"Yeah," Dave nodded, "Hugh Glass McCord. Named after the old mountain man. Called him Heck for short."

"Live there when it was a goin' town, did he?"

"Did a little cowpunchin' and even tried trapping for a while."

"Heck McCord," the sheepherder mulled the name, then shook his head. "Never was much with names. But if he ever did any drinkin' I likely knew him."

"He was known to indulge," Dave said, grinning.

Rule chuckled. "Most of us did back then. Rough town."

"This is ready," Ann said, dishing out stew into plates and handing it to them with bread. "Sorry it's not fancier," she said to Dave.

He shook his head and smiled. "Looks like a feast to me."

Bringing her plate, the girl joined them at the heater. The three of them ate in silence, and Dave found that he had to keep himself from gulping it down all at once. The stew and bread were delicious. He finished his first plate and ate another. Scraping the plate clean, he sat back and poured himself another cup of coffee.

"I don't know what was in that stew," he said with a sigh, "but I think I ought to pay to work for you."

"Thank you," Ann said shyly.

"Real good," her father nodded, handing her his plate.

"Least I can do is help wash," Dave said.

Ann took his plate. "That's woman's work," she said, collecting the rest of the dishes.

Dave watched her as she went to work pouring melted snow into a pan to use as dishwater. Asa pulled a pipe from his shirt and filled it, then held a match to it.

"Imagine your wife'll be glad to have you home," Dave said.

Rule stiffened slightly, slowly and methodically drawing smoke into his mouth.

"My wife's gone, Mr. McCord," the sheepherder said, breathing out gray, twisting whorls of smoke.

"I'm sorry."

Asa shook his head. "Not dead," he said, smiling grimly, "just gone. Left me—"

"Papa!" Ann cut in.

"It's all right. Told you that before. Nothin' to be ashamed of. Not much of a country for anything, 'specially a woman."

"I like it," Ann said hurriedly.

"Your mama didn't." Rule puffed out smoke.

"She was a—"

"Annie," her father snapped, "she done what she thought was right."

His eyes flickered self-consciously to Dave, and he pushed himself up slowly. "Think I'll take a look around," he said and, turning, pushed his way through the flap of the tent to the outside.

Dave pulled his eyes back to the girl. Her back was to him and she worked silently. He could almost feel her tension.

Frowning frustratedly, he shrugged. "Well," he said, "guess I'll go ahead and bed down. Anywhere all right?"

She nodded. "Sure."

Taking his rolled sleeping bag from the corner, he spread it on the ground, then, taking off his coat and boots, he wriggled into it and zipped it up. He watched the girl for a time, wanting to say something but not knowing what.

"Hell," he grumbled and, closing his eyes, turned away from the light and went to sleep.

Milt Chambers wiped clean the bolt of the 30.06, then laid it back down on his desk with the rest of the disassembled pieces of the rifle.

At the radio, Corey leaned on his desk, following Chambers' motions with bored eyes. "How many times you done that now?" he asked.

"Dunno," Milt replied, shrugging, "don't matter."

"All for that McCord fella."

"I'm takin' it, if that's what you mean."

Corey sniffed. "Didn't think he was all that dangerous."

"He broke arrest once, Corey. He ain't gonna do it again."

Corey shrugged and stretched back into his chair. "Goin' to a lot of trouble for nothin'."

Milt slipped the bolt back into the rifle. "Why's that?"

"You ain't gonna be able to get up that road nohow. Even in good weather, ain't nothin' but a wide place in the trees. With snow, ain't no car or jeep—"

"Not takin' the jeep," Milt said, "not all the way. Take it as far as I can go, then I'm goin' by horse."

"Oh." Corey blinked. "When you startin'?"

"In the mornin'. Givin' myself plenty of time."

"Well," Corey said, straightening in his chair, "still a helluva ride."

"I'll make it," Milt said, checking the rifle again.

Corey watched him for a moment. "Yeah," he said quietly, turning back to his radio, "I figger you will."

FIVE

Tom Quade finished saddling his horse and looked out into the pale morning. Gray blended on gray, remnants of night and snow hiding the mountains.

"Think the snow's let up a little while," the sheriff commented.

Seth looked up from the fire. "Somethin's goin' right," he said, picking up the pot. He drained the last of the coffee into two cups and handed one to the sheriff.

"How long you figure?" Tom asked, carefully sipping the hot liquid.

"Middle of the mornin', most likely," Seth said, dumping the grounds on the fire. "That is, if we get started."

Quade looked at his full cup of coffee. "Don't believe in takin' your time, do you?"

"Don't like doin' this," the old man replied, frowning. "Quicker done the better." Finishing his coffee, he took the cup and the pot to his horse and pushed them into the food sack, then took out a small bag of oats.

He fed each horse two handsful. "This is few and far between," he said to them. "You fellas are gonna have to do a little pawin'."

He put the oats back into the food sack and looked back to Quade's cup in his hand.

"We're wastin' daylight," he said.

Quade looked at his steaming cup again and, wincing, downed it. "Damn," he gasped, "keep me warm all day."

Seth smiled. "Be gone as soon as your butt hits that saddle," he said as he mounted.

Nodding, Quade followed him up, and they turned their horses out of the shelter and up the hills.

Dave McCord had been in the saddle for an hour when the first real traces of light began to drift into the dark morning.

Dogs barking dotted the crystal white blackness, echoing, mixing with the rattle of bells, then more barking, and the bleating of the sheep. His eyes stayed on the hills following them up, twisting into the morning until he couldn't see them anymore. He knew they led to the mountains but he couldn't see them. A tremor of apprehension disquieted him. The slopes were both foreign and familiar. Another country.

The rattle of hooves tugged his eyes around and Asa Rule came in beside him, smiling through his beard.

"Gettin' a case of the lonelies?"

Dave tried to smile, shaking his head. "Funny feelin' . . . kinda . . ." He shrugged, unable to explain.

Asa nodded. "I know. Like you belong and don't belong. Heard it called the fever and the lonelies, but that don't really say it. Maybe there ain't a word for it."

"Ever get used to it?"

Asa looked up and around. "Heard people say they did. Sometimes I even get to thinkin' I have." His eyes came back to Dave, skepticism brightening them. "But I've got my doubts ever once in a while. . . ." He turned his horse back toward the sheep. "Let's go to work," he said. "More we talk about it, the jumpier we're gonna be."

Pulling a horse trailer, Milt Chambers eased the jeep over to the curb in front of the sheriff's office and stopped. He left the motor running and hurried inside.

Corey looked up as the deputy came through the door.

"Headin' out, I take it?"

"Yeah." Milt nodded, going to his desk. He picked up the 30.06 on it, then the walkie-talkie and two boxes of shells. He dropped the shells into his coat pocket, slung the walkie-talkie over his shoulder with the strap, and started for the door.

"Milt," Corey said, stopping him.

The deputy looked around. "Yeah?"

"That fella you mentioned the other day . . ."

"Who's that?"

"The one that said, 'Easy don't get it done.' Sometimes it don't. Sometimes it does. Anyhow, that country out there can be mighty rough, and if I were you I'd take it a little easy—"

"I'll just have to be rougher," Chambers cut him off. "So long, Corey," he said, walking out of the office.

After stowing the 30.06 and the walkie-talkie in the rear of the jeep, Chambers climbed into the driver's seat, shifted into gear, and nosed back out onto the highway, slowly picking up speed.

Moving down the highway, the deputy lifted his eyes and looked up at the clouds, frowning. It was going to snow again. Corey was wrong. He was going to have to push like hell and then some to get to Asa's place.

"Easy don't get it done," he whispered aloud, and his hands tightened on the wheel in reflex.

Easy don't get it done.

He could still hear Sheriff Dick Hoffman saying those words. Chambers' stomach twisted hotly and he could feel again the disgust in Hoffman's eyes and voice.

Like it was happening right now instead of a year and a half ago.

It had been in Sand Wells, a small town in southern Utah. Hoffman had taken him on as a deputy and he hadn't been on the job more than a week when it all fell apart.

He and another deputy, Shorty Valdez, were taking a new prisoner from the main cell block to the showers for a mandatory sluicing down.

The prisoner, a wiry drunk named Colby, had been picked up the night before. Both Chambers and Shorty knew Colby and were giving him a good ribbing, but Colby was still wobbly and not in much of a mood for humor. Several times he told Shorty to lay off, but Shorty, still laughing, kept at it.

They reached the end of the hall and Milt ambled forward to unlock the door to the showers. He had just slipped the key in the hole when he heard the scuffling of feet. Reeling, he saw Colby diving into Shorty, pounding his fists wildly at the deputy.

Milt plunged back down the hall, getting a hold on the drunk.

"Come on now, hoss," he yelled, and tore Colby away from Shorty, stumbling backward with him. The drunk's elbow jerked back, hammering Milt in the stomach, and, still stumbling, he slammed into the wall, cracking his head against the concrete.

Dazed, Milt's grip on Colby weakened and he could feel the drunk shaking loose. Milt slumped to the floor and, shaking his head to clear it, looked up to see Colby charge into Shorty again.

Milt's hand touched the butt of the pistol at his side.

"No," he whispered, and tried to get up, but the swarming dizziness in his head pulled him back.

His hand fumbled to his gun again and he managed to tug it free of its leather.

"Colby," he barked at the drunken man, hoping to frighten him. "Goddamnit, Colby!"

Unhearing, the drunk hit Shorty again.

"Colby!" Milt shouted, but he knew it was no good.

Trembling, Milt raised the pistol. Trying to get a bead on Colby's shoulder or leg. The two men twisted, and Milt couldn't find clear shot. Not without taking the chance of killing Colby.

The gun drifted down. He knew Colby; had drunk with him. He couldn't just kill him.

Getting over on all fours, Milt began crawling for them.

He heard the clatter of boots from somewhere down the hall.

Suddenly Hoffman was there. A huge bull of a man wading into Colby, swinging a pistol, laying the drunk out cold.

Then there were more men there. They began carrying off Shorty and Colby.

Milt weaved to his feet. "Shorty all right?" he asked the sheriff.

Hoffman pivoted, facing him. "He'll be all right—no thanks to you."

Confused, Milt shook his head. "I—" he began.

"You had your gun out, why the hell didn't you use it? You shoulda used it in the first place instead of getting into it with them. Damnit, boy, he coulda killed Shorty."

Milt shook his head bewilderedly. "I'm sorry, Dick. I know Colby, I just—"

"You went easy on him," the sheriff sneered. "You gun-shy, Chambers? Learn to use that damn thing or get the hell out. You let me down, boy. Man that don't do his job ain't worth a damn. I can't depend on you." He shook his head. "Easy don't get it done. Any man worth his salt has to know that."

Then, turning away, he left Milt standing there.

The next day, when Milt came on his shift, Hoffman fired him. It had taken Milt over a year to work up enough courage to ask for another law enforcement job, and he hadn't told Quade about working in Sand Wells.

Now, driving down the highway, guiding the jeep between the banks of snow, his stomach knotted again and he could still hear Hoffman's voice.

The deputy glanced at the 30.06 in the back seat.

"Gun-shy," he whispered aloud, and could feel sweat on the back of his neck. He could use a gun as well as anybody. And do the job. Hoffman had been wrong about him. But he had learned from him. Learned a way of doing things.

The incident with Colby, then McCord . . . they had been mistakes. His fingers tightened on the plastic steering wheel. Everybody made mistakes. Everybody. It didn't mean he couldn't be depended on. He could be as good at this job as any man. Better. The next time he got the chance he would prove it.

Next time.

Riding hard, Seth led Tom Quade down a run of rugged hills, edging east and away from the mountains.

It was close to ten o'clock when the two men drew their horses in on a high plateau. Below, the land stretched away from them like a white chasm.

"There," Seth said, pointing off to the north.

Squinting to see, Tom Quade frowned and finally shook his head.

"Just what the hell am I looking at?"

"Asa and his sheep."

Quade stared skeptically at the old man. "You mean you can really see something out there?"

"Asa and his sheep," Seth repeated, grinning. "Sure some of that fat ain't gettin' in your eyes?"

Tom ignored him. "How far away?"

"Ten, fifteen miles."

Quade looked again. He gave up and frowned. "All I can see is white."

Seth smiled. "Sheep are white, Tom."

"You old bastard, I know what the hell color they are. How long?"

Seth rubbed his chin. "Four hours at the outside."

Nodding wearily, Tom began to turn his horse down the long rise.

"This way," Seth called, heading out down a small column of rocks. "Blind canyon down there."

Quade pulled his horse around, grumbling.

"Seth?"

"What?"

"Ah . . . hell, nothin', goddamnit."

As noon approached, Ann Rule rode on ahead of the herd and set up a quick camp in an aspen grove. The snow had stopped, but thick clouds sealed the sky and a chill breeze clicked the naked white limbs and scraps of leaves. Working hurriedly, Ann prepared the lunch, then walked back to the edge of the trees. The first of the herd had already started past her and she could see her father and Dave McCord.

She touched her fair hair, smoothing it back slightly. She found herself suddenly wishing that she had a dress to wear.

"Now that's silly," she snapped aloud as soon as she realized the thought. "Silly . . ." she whispered.

Jeans and woolen were the best thing for this country. A dress was impractical.

Shaking her head, she turned and walked back to the portable stove. Why was she thinking so much about Dave McCord? she wondered. At seventeen, she had never been out with a boy, but she had talked to them. Looking back at Dave riding into camp, she wondered if that was it. The way he talked to her—not like she was something for listening and impressing, but as a person who had something in her mind besides cooking and babies.

Dismounting, the men hitched their horses.

"Ready, honey," her father called.

Blinking, she looked up. "What? Oh, yes," she said, and quickly served it to them.

Dave ate ravenously. The hot beans, beef, and coffee were like a missing part of him that he had finally found. He went through two heaping platesful, then sat by the fire, thinking about asking for a third.

"More there," Asa said after eyeing him for a moment.

"No," Dave protested weakly, "I, ah . . ."

Asa smiled. "You're a reasonably good hand. At least worth what you can eat."

Dave reflected his grin. "I wouldn't bet on that. Right now I feel like I could duck my head in a bucket of it." He looked up at Ann. "You're a darn fine cook."

"Thank you," she said shyly.

Dave helped himself to another plateful and a cup of coffee. "Why is it you winter up here?" he asked Asa.

"Good pasture," the sheepherder answered.

"Thought you'd take 'em lower down."

Asa shook his head. "This valley's set pretty low and protected. Foggy Peak's above it, and the ridges around it are darn near circular. That cut in the mountains leads over to the west side, but after the snow flies it fills up. Actually hardly no snow at all in the valley."

"Sounds like a good place," Dave said.

"It is," Asa said. "It's home."

When they were finished all three helped clean up. In the saddle, Asa fell back to Dave.

"Just wanted to say," he began difficultly, glancing back toward his daughter, "that Annie—well, she didn't mean to get fired up about her ma last night. She's a little touchy, that's all."

Dave nodded. "I think I understand."

"She's a good girl," Rule said. "Oughta be findin' her a man. Seein' a little of the world. Don't know why she stays up here," he cleared his throat self-consciously, "and I don't know why I talk so damn much." He started to turn his horse out.

"Asa," Dave called.

The sheepherder held up. "Yeah?"

"Oh," Dave shrugged, "just thanks for takin' me in. Glad I'm of some help."

The sheepherder looked back at him for a moment. "You know, son," he said, "I wasn't gonna say nothin', but—"

Dave tensed slightly. "What?"

Rule shook his head. "Not quite sure, really. You just don't act like you mind bein' lost out here."

Dave attempted a smile and looked up ahead. "Much further to your place?"

Asa shrugged his shoulders. "If you don't want to talk about it, that's your affair. . . . Tomorrow night," he answered the question. "Late."

"And, Asa . . ."

"Yeah?"

"Thanks again."

The sheepherder nodded slowly. "You're welcome, son," he said, and went back to the sheep.

Coming over a sharp hogback, Seth saw the herd below them. He pulled Nate in quickly, easing away from the crest, motioning to Tom to halt.

"Asa's to the rear," the old rancher said. "McCord is forward. Annie's about halfway back."

Quade nodded slowly, his mouth pressed in thought.

"He still have the rifle?"

"He has it," Seth said, nodding.

"Damn," the sheriff grumbled. "After his run-in with Milt, I want to go at him careful. I don't think he'd use that gun, but then again he might. Always have to suppose that he will."

"Yeah." Seth nodded. "And if he sees us, he's liable to break for it. He knows me."

"Well," the sheriff sighed, "ain't no easy way of doin' it."

Seth shifted in the saddle. "One maybe," he said slowly, thinking the words through. "We could follow till nightfall, and come in on him in camp. Darkness would cover us."

Quade smiled. "You know," he said, "you're still awful good at this job. Some things you don't forget, I guess."

The old man's face hardened slightly. "No," he frowned, "some things you don't."

Milt Chambers rammed the jeep as far up the slope as it would go, then slacked off, letting it roll back a little.

"Damn," he barked, hitting the wheel angrily. Jerking it down into low, he gunned it, bolting back up the slope, the motor straining, tires screaming into the snow and mud. But he wasn't going anywhere.

Slamming in the clutch, Chambers let the jeep roll back again.

"Bastard," he whispered, trembling. Kicking open the door, he stepped out.

It was colder than he had expected. The warmth of the jeep had lulled him. Shivering, he examined the tires, then the slope. Turning, he kicked the front tire, then hunched back into the jeep's cab.

After he'd warmed himself again he pushed back out into the cold and walked back to the horse trailer.

Opening the gate, he backed the horse out, tightened the cinch, then led him back to the cab. Gathering up the food sack and walkie-talkie, he put them around either side of the saddle horn, then lifted out the box of shells and the rifle. The shells he put in his pocket, the rifle into its boot.

Mounting the horse, he looked up the dark slopes into the heavy clouds sifting through the trees.

His hands trembled slightly and he grasped the reins tighter.

He would make it, he nodded, kicking the horse out, running the animal as hard as he could.

He would make it. He had to.

Seth Mattick dismounted and, slipping along the top of a ridge, peered at the mass of sheep through the beginning haze of twilight. Moving his eyes forward, he was able to make out two people ahead of the herd, setting up camp.

McCord and Ann Rule.

Stepping back to his horse, Seth trotted him back down to the waiting sheriff.

"Another thirty minutes," the old man said, nodding. "Then it'll be dark enough to ride right up to him."

"Funny," Dave McCord said, hesitating, glancing up from the tent peg he was hammering into the ground.

Ann Rule looked up. "What?"

"Thought I saw somethin'," he said. "On that ridge out there."

Ann followed his gaze through the coming twilight, then, smiling, shook her head. "The fever. You're seein' things."

"Maybe." McCord shrugged uneasily, then went back to setting up the tent. When they finished they went inside and Ann started the heater and stove. Pulling up a folding chair, he warmed his hands and watched the girl starting dinner.

"You ever get it?" he asked.

Ann glanced at him. "What?"

"The fever."

She smiled. "Sometimes," she admitted.

Dave rubbed his hands together, holding them out to the heater.

"You been up here long?"

"Lived here, you mean?" She rustled her shoulders. "Most of my life."

"You like it?"

She regarded him quietly for a moment, then shrugged. "Yes, I suppose. My father needs me here."

"Oh." Dave nodded. "What about later? You think you'll get a job or go to school? Something like that?"

"I . . . don't know," she answered slowly. "I really haven't thought about it. I'll let Papa decide—he makes all the decisions. I'd just as soon stay here. He's more important than all that."

"Yeah." Dave smiled grimly. "Fathers have a way of being important." He looked up at her. "You ever been anyplace but Three Medicine?"

"Laramie," she said as she filled a pan with water and placed it on a burner. "But it was a long time ago." Stooping, she opened a sack of potatoes and began taking some from it, placing them on the table. "I've read a lot, though, about places like Madrid, Paris, London—"

"London is a good city." Dave nodded. "I can't say that I liked the others much."

Ann turned. "You've been there?" she asked excitedly. "To all those places?"

Dave smiled, embarrassed. "I've been there," he admitted. "But not really to know them. Except London. I had some days free while my father was finalizing a deal for some Arab oil."

Ann's eyes changed, calmed. "You must be very wealthy," she said, starting to peel the potatoes.

"My father is," Dave corrected her.

"Did you travel with him much?"

Dave nodded. "Quite a bit."

"Didn't that interfere with your schooling?"

A slow, humorless smile began on his lips. "That was my schooling. My father's idea of schooling." The smile hardened. "The Harlin Marcus McCord School of Self-Made Men." Dave glanced at her self-consciously. "I'm afraid the kind of business he was teaching wasn't being taught in schools."

"I don't understand. What kind of business?"

Dave shook his head. "Not any one kind—the way it was done. Ways of using people against themselves. If a man has a mistress you let him know you know. If a competitor has a blemish on his record, you leak it in a way that's most harmful to him. Alter it slightly. Even if he can prove it was a lie, the harm's been done. My father was very good at that. There are other things, too. Several times he raised the price of crude oil, saying it was to cover the cost of shipping or labor or the like. But say the costs amounted to ten per cent, he would raise them thirty. Twenty more per cent for him. Every time there was a strike and he had to raise wages, he made money. Sometimes he instigated them. 'When you can see an inch, take a mile,' he used to say. When customers would complain, he would just say, 'Look at my costs, they've gone up, too.' Of course, he made sixty per cent more profit last year than the year before. That was the kind of business I was learning."

Hesitating, Ann looked at him for a long time. "I just can't see you doing that kind of thing."

"It's easier than you think." Dave frowned. "I'd probably still be at it if it weren't for my grandfather."

"The man you talked about last night. Heck?"

Dave nodded, smiling. "Old Heck," he whispered, then his eyes darkened. "Hard to believe they were father and son. Heck was a drifter. Cowhand. Mountain man. Even a gun runner once. Five years ago my father talked him into taking over one of his ranches—"

"Giving somebody a ranch isn't exactly selfish," Ann cut in.

"No," Dave acknowledged, "but the reasons are always what's important. I think it embarrassed him having a father who was a bum, just a cup of coffee from being broke. A failure, to his way of thinking." Dave shrugged. "I suppose he cared for Heck, and for me in his own way, wanting what he thought was best for me. Thing of it was, he never gave me a chance to think of what was best for me."

"And Heck changed that?" Ann asked.

Dave nodded. "It was the difference in them that brought it home to me. I spent as much time as I could with Heck in the last five years." He smiled in memory. "Our last hunting trip was to Grass River." The smile softened. "Good times . . ." he whispered. "I remember one day, late in the evening, after Heck and I had hiked around the lower hills, we built a fire on the ridge overlooking a line of trees where the mountains come down to what's left of the town. Sitting there, we watched the darkness come. The mountains looked like a part of someplace else and Heck got to talking about them. How he'd hunted them when he was young, then again only a few years before. Even built a cabin and left it stocked, meaning to come back. Then my father had offered him the ranch—"

"There's a cabin in those mountains?" Ann interrupted.

"Deep in the wilderness." Dave nodded. "He talked about it and his voice was soft, like he was talking about a woman. 'Got half a mind to go back,' he said, and I asked him why he didn't. He looked away from me, but I could see a hint of wet in his eyes. 'Don't belong there no more,' he said."

Ann looked up. "Didn't belong?"

Dave nodded.

"Why?"

Dave shook his head. "I don't know. He was up and walking before I had a chance to ask him. Later, down in Grass River, he put me off saying he'd tell me some other time. The next day Heck went down to Three Medicine to pick up my father, who was supposed to join us. I decided to stay in Grass River, and I was alone there for two days. I walked back out to that ridge more than once. Looking at the stand of trees and the beginning of the high country, wondering what was up there. What it was like on the other side of that first line of trees, then the next one. I thought about Heck's cabin, and what time alone in the mountains would be like.

"I came down from the ridge pretty late the evening of the second day. My father was there and he was mad as hell. He was flying to Argentina to buy some cattle and he wanted me to come along. He had wanted to go back to Three Medicine that afternoon, but my getting back so late had fouled that up.

"I told him I wanted to go into the mountains instead. Spend some time alone. He exploded. Said it was the craziest thing he'd ever heard; there were important things to be taken care of and there was no time for daydreaming and useless activity. I told him I'd do it anyway. For a moment I thought he was going to get angrier. He didn't. Instead, he laughed, saying I would do as I was told. That I always had and always would. That I was weak and didn't have the guts to go against him and be on my own."

Dave frowned, silent for a moment. "We stayed the night in Grass River. I must have walked back to that ridge and the line of trees ten times that night. Even readied a horse once." He shook his head. "But I couldn't do it."

"Why?"

Dave shrugged. "I don't really know. They just scared the hell out of me. Maybe because of what was beyond them. Or that I'd be on my own—absolutely on my own for the first time. No one to help me.

"I went to the cabin Heck was using and asked him to help me. He said he couldn't. When it came time I'd have to do it alone." The young man frowned. "We left the next morning. I never made it to those trees or the cabin."

Ann finished with the potatoes and put the last in the water on the stove. "That cabin," she said, turning to him. "Has that got something to do with why you're out here?" She smiled suddenly. "Papa likes you, but he's a little skeptical about your being lost out here . . . and I am, too. . . ."

Standing, Dave started to deny it, then, seeing no use in it, he nodded. "That's part of it," he admitted.

Ann's smile faded. "Dave, are you in some kind of trouble?"

The young man attempted a smile. "No," he said, then gestured toward the flap. "I'd better see to the rest of the supplies."

"Dave," Ann said.

Hesitating, he looked back at her.

"I . . . think your grandfather would be proud of you," she said.

His eyes darkened. "I hope so," he said, his jaw hardening. "I'll never know. He died six months ago," he whispered, and hurriedly pushed through the flap and outside.

White darkness had come and it felt good to the young man. He walked toward the sheep and stopped, looking out over the herd when he saw the rider coming toward him.

"Asa," he called.

No answer. The rider kept coming. A shadow in the darkness. A few yards from him now.

He started to call again, then realized that it wasn't just one man, but two.

Turning, he started to run, but stopped before he could move.

Seth Mattick stepped from behind the tent. There was a rifle in his hands. It was leveled at Dave.

"Mattick? What—"

The old rancher frowned. "It's over, son," he said.

SIX

At her stove, Ann heard the sound of voices. More than just her father and Dave. Somebody else was out there.

Turning, she was starting for the opening when Dave pushed back through the tent flap.

"Dave?" she said, then saw the gunbarrel behind him. Then Seth Mattick followed him in. Then Tom Quade and her father.

Her eyes jerked to Dave in confusion. "What—"

"Seems we got a fugitive on our hands," Asa said to her, an edge of anger in his voice. "Slugged a deputy back in Three Medicine."

Ann looked to Dave as Seth sat him down in a canvas chair. "Why?" she asked unbelievingly.

"Time for that later," her father cut in brusquely. "Right now these men need some coffee and I better get the rest of the supplies in."

"I'll help you," Quade said. "Need to see to our horses. He glanced at Dave. "And get that rifle off his saddle."

"Asa," Dave looked up from his chair, "I—"

The sheepherder looked at him. "Son," he frowned, "I got nothin' against you. Matter of fact you helped out quite a bit. Just figger you lied to me. Let me work my mad off about that."

Turning, the sheepherder pushed through the flap and outside, Quade following.

Seth smiled wearily at the young man. "Might as well take it easy, son," the old man said.

Frowning, Dave settled back into his chair, his silence weighting through him, and Seth turned to Ann. She was still staring at the young man.

"Could use that coffee," he said.

Ann's eyes jerked up and, nodding absently, she turned back to the stove, poured him a cup, then began fixing another pot.

Asa and Quade began bringing things inside.

"How close is supper?" Asa asked.

"Not long," she answered, and found that she had to concentrate to get anything done at the stove. She poured coffee for her father and the sheriff, and as they sat down with it around the heater, she finished cooking the meal and served it up.

They ate in clumsy silence.

Seth finished his plate and sipped his coffee uncomfortably. He watched McCord piece through his food, then put it, half finished, back on the table near the stove.

Standing, Seth took the coffeepot from the stove and warmed his cup, then looked at the young man.

"You want to tell us about it, son?"

The lines around Dave's mouth tauted. "What good'd it do?"

Seth shrugged. "Don't know," the old man admitted. "Folks back there care about you."

Dave's eyes came up and he smiled grimly. "I know. That's why I'm out here."

"They put out three thousand dollars for information for you," Quade put in. "Somebody sure as hell cares."

Dave blinked, surprised. "Three thousand," he said, then nodded knowingly. "Yeah, he would."

"Who?" Quade asked.

"My father," Dave answered.

"Something wrong with that?"

Dave shrugged. "You'd have to know my father." He frowned and shook his head. "What the hell," he said, sighing. "I don't owe you any explanations."

Seth nodded toward Asa and Ann. "You might owe them one," he said.

Dave raised his eyes. He looked at Asa, then at Ann. His eyes softened. "Yeah," he conceded, "I guess I might at that." He looked back to the sheepherder. "Asa, you're right. I lied to you and I'm sorry about it."

Asa frowned, shrugging reluctantly. "No harm done, I reckon."

Dave held out his cup and Ann poured him more coffee. "What I told you earlier," he said to her, "I wasn't lying then."

"I know." She nodded.

Dave looked at Seth. "What do you want to know?"

The old man shrugged. "How come you to be in that hospital?"

A grim smile pressed Dave's lips. "My father and I had a difference of opinion."

Quade cut in, "Your father confined you to a hospital over a difference of opinion?"

"In a manner of speaking," Dave replied, nodding. "Six months," he said, swallowing tightly, and Seth saw a tremor in his hands.

"Why?" Seth asked.

"Lot of reasons." Dave sighed, then seemed lost in thought for a moment. "We've been at odds for the past few years. More so after a hunting trip up to Grass River—the one I told you about, Ann," he said, and related it quickly to the others.

"That trip," he went on, "affected the relationship between me and my father more deeply than either of us realized. That was when we really began to split. I began leaving his way of thinking and going over to Heck's.

"I spent a lot of time out at Heck's ranch. Got to know a lot of people around there. One of them was a man named Ben Terrill. Owned the ranch next to Heck's." Dave smiled. "He was crusty as hell. Nearly a hermit. Jealous about his land. Wouldn't even let anybody have a drink of water off it.

"Took him a couple of years to get around to speaking to Heck. Then they became fast friends. Even rented Heck some of his pastureland. And because I was Heck's grandson, he took a shine to me.

"Then last spring my father had some oil-survey work done. The geologist thought the Terrill pasture was ours, and he went over it, too. He told my father that the best chance for oil in the region was on that pasture.

"We were having dinner that night when my father brought it up. Said that since we were friends of Terrill's we might be able to get the pasture from him, mineral rights and all. He would pay Terrill twice what the property was worth as pasture. Terrill would make money. And we would make money. Everyone would come out ahead.

"I'll never forget Heck sitting there at the kitchen table as my father talked. When he finished, Heck's eyes came up and he looked older than I'd ever seen him. Like a hundred years had caught up with him in my father's voice.

"Shaking with rage, he told my father to get out. My father shook his head calmly and said that Heck was in no position to be telling him to do anything. The house and the land were half his.

"Heck exploded out of the chair, starting for my father, then suddenly his hand fluttered to his chest and he was falling. . . ." Dave's voice lapsed into quiet and he stared at the floor.

"His heart?" Seth asked.

Dave nodded. " 'Massive coronary,' the doctors said. My father had him taken to a private hospital. Heck knew he was dying. He begged my father to let him go back to the ranch so he could die there. Near the mountains. My father said that was stupid. He would stay there. Nothing but the best for Harlin McCord's father."

The young man trembled, struggling to control his voice. "Heck died the evening of the second day. He was in bed. Under an oxygen tent. Only an outline in the sheets. His breathing made a rasping sound. His head drifted and he looked at me, the same way he had that night on the ridge above Grass River. 'Make your ride, boy,' he whispered. 'I hope you make it to the trees. . . .'

"And he was gone."

Dave's voice drifted. The wind riddled the walls of the tent.

"Dave . . ." Ann probed.

"Yeah," he said, nodded, and began again. "I called for the doctors, but there was nothing they could do. They took Heck away and I was still sitting in his room when my father came. He began talking about a trip he had planned. First Algeria, then Spain. I told him no. That I was finished. He grabbed me and slapped me, telling me I would do as I was told like I'd always done. That's when I hit him. Then people were all over me. I was knocked unconscious.

"When I woke up I was in one of the rooms. My father said I was going to stay there until I came to my senses. Since I was twenty—underage—there was nothing I could do.

"I spent six months in that place," Dave said, and Seth watched the young man's fingers tighten around the cup he was holding, pressing hard into the tin. "Most of it was in that room. It was like being in limbo—not living at all.

"I thought my father was playing some kind of game. That he would let me go soon, and all I had to do was wait him out. I did everything I could to pass time. But you can only read so many books, or watch so much television. I wanted to be outside. The longer I was there the more I thought about the mountains, and Heck's cabin in the Wild Horse Range. It seemed to be the only real thing I could get hold of. Sometimes I think it was the only reason I didn't go crazy.

"My father came several times. Every time, he reminded me of how much the Terrill deal could be worth. Five million, maybe more. He would say it over and over. The last time I saw him was three months ago. He asked me again to try this thing with Terrill. I told him to go to hell. He left saying he wouldn't be back. If I wanted out, I'd have to call him."

The young man lifted his eyes to Seth's. "I think he really believes I'm crazy. That I'd have to be to pass up money like that. Somethin' he's spent a lifetime trying to gain. More than that, he has to prove I'm crazy, because if I'm not, then it's him that's wrong. His whole way of life is wrong . . . and I don't think he can live with that. Winning is everything to him. Winning means being right. Survival. That was the reason I was in the hospital.

"Like I said, I thought it was a game, that all I had to do was wait him out. When he didn't come back for two months, I knew it wasn't a game. At least not a simple one.

"When I realized that I began to think seriously of the only other way out. Escape. It was the only way I had.

"Heck's cabin in the wilderness became even more important to me then. It was one place my father couldn't get to me. If I could beat my fear and make it past that line of trees, then I could beat him, too.

"Getting out of the hospital wasn't hard, not once I made up my mind to it. It just took time.

"I made friends with a male nurse. Got access to the room where he and some of the others changed clothes, and stole a uniform. I walked out carrying a bundle of laundry.

"I went back to the ranch and put together my gear. I told the foreman I was headed south, then went into town, drew the money out of an account there, and headed north. I bought a car in Laramie under another name, and came up here."

Seth nodded. "And you had your run-in with Milt Chambers back in Three Medicine."

"Yeah," Dave frowned, sighing. "I saw him come into that cafe and all I could think about was going back to the hospital." His fingers grasped the cup again, whitening with pressure.

"Maybe," Seth shrugged, "maybe he's changed his mind. You might work something out."

Dave shook his head. "No," he said, "I've cut myself off. In one way at least. I wrote Terrill and told him about the oil on his land. What choice would I have had anyway? I would have had to cheat a man to get out." The young man finished his coffee and placed the cup on the table. "Now he'll be sure I'm crazy. He'll keep me there until I break. The only way out will be on his terms. . . ." The lines in his jaw hardened. "And I can't do that . . . what I do has to be on my terms. Win or lose, it has to be on my terms."

A quiet echo of fear twisted through Seth's stomach.

Dave wearily leaned forward on his knees, then looked to Quade. "I'll turn in now, if it's all right with you."

"Yeah," the sheriff said, nodding. "Go ahead."

Dave lifted himself from his chair and crossed to his bedroll.

Standing, Asa pulled on his coat. "Better have another look around," he said. He started for the door, then looked back at Dave. "About your lyin' to me . . ."

Dave turned.

"We're square," the sheepherder said, then pushed through the flap and outside.

Dave's eyes lingered on the opening for a moment, then looked to Ann.

"How 'bout you?" he asked.

The girl nodded. "Me too," she said, then shrugged. "I just wish there was something I could do."

Dave grinned. "Smuggle me a file," he said, and the smile faded. "Good night." He nodded and turned to his sleeping bag.

Ann started to say something else, then, shrugging, began to do the dishes.

As the young man climbed into his bag, Quade reached into his back pocket. He pulled out a pair of handcuffs and stared at them.

Seth glanced at them, then back to his coffee.

Quade frowned. "Well, he broke arrest."

"That's right," Seth agreed.

Sighing, the frown deepened on the sheriff's lips. "Family trouble, it sounds like. . . ."

Seth didn't say anything. Bringing up his cup, he sipped his coffee.

"Suppose I could sleep by the door tonight," Quade went on. "Tomorrow we could stick pretty close to him." He shook his head. "'Sides, I think he's had enough and I hate to add to it." He looked at Seth.

The old man was smiling.

"Think I'm gettin' soft, don't you?"

Seth shook his head. "No."

"Well, I am," the sheriff grumbled, and, getting up, he went to the stove for more coffee.

Still smiling, the old rancher's eyes came back to the young man on the sleeping bag. The smile darkened. There was something about that boy . . . something . . .

"Gonna take a turn outside," he said to Quade and, buttoning his coat, he pushed through the flap. The harsh, cold air felt good against his face. The tent was big enough, but it had gotten awfully close in there suddenly. And there was something about McCord. Almost like he could feel him breathing.

He walked around the tent to the tarp shelter that had been rigged for the horses and checked Nate and the other mounts.

Starting back to the tent, he hesitated, gazing up where he knew the mountains were, thinking that he would have the money to make it through now, and keep his place. He would be all right, but he wondered about McCord.

"None of my trouble," the old man whispered aloud. He had just done his job. There was nothing wrong in that.

Frowning, he shook his head. Then he wondered why didn't he feel better about it.

Dave watched Seth come back into the tent and pour himself more coffee. In front of the door, Quade was putting down his bedroll.

The young man's eyes pulled back and he stared at the canvas ceiling, which was trembling with the wind.

There has to be a way, he thought desperately. And remembering the hospital, his throat tightened, pressing an ache through his chest, cording the muscles in his stomach.

There still had to be a way to those trees.

There had to be, because he wasn't going back.

SEVEN

Fragments of dark sunlight scattered over the snow as Seth, Tom, and Asa emerged from the tent into the cold morning.

"Been a lotta wolf signs around," the sheepherder said. "Think I'll get to work." He slapped Quade on the belly. "Ride with me awhile, and I'll get rid of that for you."

Smiling, Quade sighed. "Ain't an easy life havin' a gut." He looked to Seth. "You want to watch McCord this mornin'?"

"Fine." The old rancher nodded, watching as Quade and Asa went to their horses, saddled them, and rode out.

Pushing back inside, Seth found that Ann had finished packing most of the cooking gear. McCord carried a sack to the doorway and looked at the old rancher.

"All right if I take this out?" he asked. There was no anger in his voice.

"Sure." Seth nodded and the young man slipped by him.

"Anything else?" Seth asked Ann. She handed him two more sacks and, carrying the portable stove herself, they went outside. The three of them brought the tent down and finished breaking camp.

Taking McCord's rifle from his own gear, Seth unloaded it and broke it down into two pieces, then tied it on to one of the pack animals. After looking over the gear, he frowned and handed McCord's food sack and saddlebags back to the young man.

"Have to carry those yourself," he said. "These pack animals have got enough to tote."

Dave smiled vaguely. "The .30-30 wouldn't be any trouble."

Seth's mouth creased. "Nice of you to offer, but they can manage."

They finished tying the gear on the two pack animals, then saddled their mounts and moved out.

"Last of sleepin' in a tent for a while," Seth said to Ann.

She nodded. "Be home tonight." She smiled, then, looking at Dave, the smile faded.

"Dave," she said, "it might work out all right. Maybe you're wrong. He could have changed. . . ."

"No." Dave shook his head. "I've got to beat him first. Maybe then he'll leave me alone. I know him too well. I know what he's like." He looked to Seth. "How long before we get back?"

"Four, maybe five days," Seth answered.

Dave nodded. "Six days back to the hospital . . ." His hands tightened on the saddle horn and he glanced back again. Dave nudged his sorrel out and reined in again twenty yards ahead.

Ann looked to Seth. "What will happen to him, Mr. Mattick?"

Seth shook his head. "I don't know."

"He's got a right to be free."

"Yeah." The old man frowned darkly. "It's just not that simple anymore."

Deputy Milt Chambers pushed hard up the long slope and, topping a rise, he lifted his eyes to Foggy Peak looming above him.

"Not far now," he said, breathing heavily. Ten or fifteen miles, he reasoned.

Looking south, he squinted, trying to make out any movement. There was none. Frowning, he reached down and picked up the walkie-talkie, then pressed the button.

"Tom, this is Milt. Over."

No answer. The wind moved in the trees.

He pressed the button again. "Tom, this is Milt. Over."

Releasing the button, he listened, and finally shook his head.

They might have gone over the mountains, he thought. It didn't matter, he told himself. He'd wanted to have a hand in bringing McCord in, but at least he'd done his job this time. Nobody could say he hadn't.

Seth spotted Foggy Peak just before noon.

"We're comin' in," he said to Ann.

The girl brought her eyes around from Dave, still ahead of them. "What?" she said absently. "Oh, yes." She smiled. "Guess I'd better start thinking about lunch."

"Best news I've had all day," Seth said, grinning.

Riding forward, they picked up Dave, then went on to a cut between the hills. Ann set up her portable stove and began fixing hot beans and coffee.

Tom and Asa rode in as she was serving it up. There were deep lines of worry in Asa's face as he took his plate.

"You look like somebody just told you you're gonna have to go bear huntin' with nothin' but a bucket of water," Seth said to the sheepherder.

A light grin pushed at Asa's troubled lips. "Feel like it. Wolves got a couple last night."

"Sorry," Seth replied, frowning.

"Wouldn't even be this bad, but so much of the small game's been poisoned or died off this summer. Now we got a winter that looks like it would make the Pope drink."

"Or make me get religion," Seth said with a nod.

They finished their meal without saying much else, then returned the plates and got back in the saddle. Seth and McCord moved out and Quade and Asa rode to the opposite side of the herd.

Ann finished her chores and loaded the cooking equipment back on the pack horses. Looking forward, she could see Dave McCord and Seth in the distance.

"Damn," she whispered and, turning to her horse, she mounted and followed the sheep.

The longer she rode, the more it worked on her mind. She could think of nothing else.

It was mid-afternoon when her father rode in beside her.

"Got any of that coffee left?"

Pulling a thermos from the food sack on one of the pack animals, she poured it for him.

"Thank you, honey," he said, taking the cup. Following her gaze to McCord and Seth, he cleared his throat. "What is it about that fella, anyway?"

Starting, Ann's eyes came to her father's. "What?"

Asa pointed with his coffee cup. "That young fella, McCord. He's got you pretty well riled. I was just wonderin' why."

"Nothing." She shook her head.

"Annie," her father reproached her softly, "keepin' things ain't the way you and me do it."

"No," she said, shaking her head. "I guess it isn't. I just feel confused, Papa. I never thought about things like bein' free before, but now they seem important to me." She looked at her father. "And I feel beholdin' to him, like I owe him somethin'. It's silly, isn't it?"

Asa frowned deeply. "No." He shook his head. "It's not silly. You'll always feel that way about folks that teach you somethin' or give you a new idea."

"He's got a right to his own life, Papa."

"That's right, honey, he has." Asa nodded. "But I think you'd better stay out of this. You're just gonna get upset for nothin'." He finished his coffee and handed the cup back to her. "Now do as I say." He touched her cheek gently. "I'm gonna see if the others want some coffee. Why don't you find a spot," he said, turning his horse out.

Halting, Ann watched her father ride out. She frowned deeply, her fingernails digging into her gloves as she gripped the pommel of the saddle.

Sometimes she didn't know what was right or wrong. She always left that up to her father. But now she knew one thing.

She was going to help Dave McCord if she could.

EIGHT

A few miles away from Foggy Peak, Milt Chambers pulled his horse in. Picking up the walkie-talkie, he pressed the "send" button.

"Tom? This is Milt. Over."

Releasing the button, he waited. Getting no answer, he tried again.

He listened. The wind eased through the trees. Above him, clouds blending, parting, then opening again, rushing across the sky.

Frowning, he started to put the radio back when a voice cracked through.

". . . ilt. Tom . . . 'ver."

Smiling, he jerked the radio back to his mouth.

"Tom? Milt. You got him?"

"Aff . . . itive. Wait . . . cabin. . . . Out."

"Roger, and out." The deputy laughed and dropped the radio back down to let it hang from the saddle horn.

They got the bastard, he said to himself, nodding. Hope I get a little time alone with him.

"Hup," he said to the horse, and started for Asa's cabin.

Dave McCord watched Foggy Peak, and the steep hills below it, materializing out of the clouds. He had been able to see the mountain since this morning, but it was becoming a reality now. Like the old man beside him. Taking him back.

The sound of hooves pulled his eyes around. Quade crossed the sheep and drew in beside Seth.

"Milt's here," the sheriff said, smiling.

Frowning, Dave looked forward.

"Looks like we're about to the barn," Seth said with a nod.

"Looks like Milt's finally doin' somethin' right," Quade said.

Asa rode in behind them. "I see you talkin' on that thing?" The sheepherder pointed at the radio.

"Deputy," Quade said. "He'll be up at your place soon."

Asa nodded. "Better ride back and tell Annie, then. Told her to stop for coffee, but I guess you won't be wantin' to."

"The hell I don't." Quade cocked his head, turning his horse. "I don't see how you keep from freezin' your can off out here."

Asa, Seth, and McCord turned.

"Don't," replied Asa. "Ain't you ever noticed how skinny I am back there. 'Course now, you, it'd take a blizzard . . .'"

"All right." Quade frowned. "Tell you what I think we'll do, though. Either Seth or me'll take McCord on to the cabin after we have that coffee."

Asa looked to Seth. "You remember the way?"

"East around the hills, keeping an eye on Foggy."

Asa nodded. "Just stay out of that canyon."

Dave's eyes came up.

"Why's that?" Quade asked.

Asa glanced self-consciously at Dave. "Because you'll end up on the other side of the mountains if you do. Canyon leads straight to the cut through the range."

Dave looked back over his shoulder, then slowly to Seth.

"That close?" he said.

The old rancher frowned. "That close." He nodded.

Seeing the men coming in, Ann started to pour the coffee.

"Smells good," her father said, grinning as he eagerly dismounted. Seth and Tom followed him down.

Still in the saddle, Dave reined in his horse and, putting his weight on his left foot to dismount, he realized that he was the only one still mounted.

He looked from Seth to Quade to Asa. Joking.

Ann pouring coffee.

For a fraction of a second longer they wouldn't notice him.

He looked back at the hills and made his decision in movement, not thought, twisting the sorrel around.

On the ground, Ann saw him move and, suddenly dropping the thermos and cup she was holding, shouted, screaming at the horses. Scattering them as Dave pivoted his horse, running.

Quade's horse reeled into Quade, slamming him to the ground.

Ann was still shouting.

The horses were crow-hopping, jackhammering their feet backward and away.

Scrambling to his feet, Quade dived for his horse, clutching the saddle horn.

Seth dropped his cup, trying to keep hold of Nate's reins, but Quade's horse rammed a shoulder into him, sprawling him into the snow.

In the saddle, Dave was running. Shouting and waving her hat, Ann was scattering her horse, Seth's, and Asa's.

Exploding off the ground, Seth charged the girl, tackling her, hauling her down, rolling in the snow.

With one hand still on the saddle horn, Quade hugged himself to his reeling animal and knew he wasn't going to make it. Reaching across the saddle with his free hand, he tried to pull himself up, but the frantic wheeling of his horse loosened his grip and he could feel himself falling. Groping desperately, he closed his hand around the strap of the walkie-talkie. The horse reared again and, still holding the walkie-talkie, Quade tumbled, slamming into the snow. Turning, he could see Dave giving his horse its head, leaning forward in the saddle, headed for Foggy Peak.

Quade pushed himself to his feet and, watching the man run, he trembled.

"Goddamnit," Seth heard him whisper, then roar in frustration, "Goddamnit to hell, that's what I get for bein' softhearted." He looked at Ann on the ground. "What the hell were you doin'?" Not waiting for an answer, he jerked the walkie-talkie from the snow.

"Milt," he snapped. "Come in, goddamnit, Milt."

The voice on the walkie-talkie startled Chambers. He pulled in his horse on the hill above Asa's cabin and answered.

"Chambers, here."

". . . caped. . . . Intercept . . ."

"Say again."

". . . Cord . . . escaped. . . . 'cept . . ." The voice cracked and faded.

"Which way?"

No answer.

"Tom?"

He waited for a moment, then, swearing, put the radio back down, hanging from the saddle horn. He remembered Seth saying something about crossing the mountains near here. Looking to the south end of the valley, the deputy could see the spine of the mountains falling away.

Kicking his horse out, Chambers pushed down through the long valley below Foggy Peak. There was little snow on the valley floor and the deputy made good time.

He topped the hill at the south end of the valley and drew his horse in. The cut through the mountains dropped to the west. Below him, coming up from the south, was a long canyon running into the cut.

I've got him, Chambers thought, smiling, then, easing down the hill, rode along the rim of the canyon. The walls fell away beneath him at nearly a sheer angle.

There was no way down.

The smile faded from the deputy's mouth. His eyes moved frantically over the rim.

Dismounting, he edged to the top of the wall, his boots slipping in the snow. The snow gave under him a little and, catching himself with one hand, he pulled himself back up. The damn rim was steep. He'd have to watch it. Turning, he climbed into the saddle, twisting the horse back the way they'd come.

Right now he had to find a way down. Goddamnit, there had to be one or the bastard would get away from him again.

Dave ran his sorrel hard toward the steep hills and, seeing the canyon mouth, he turned the horse toward it.

The walls rushed up around him, imprisoning the sound of his running, echoing it back on him.

He wound through the channel of rock for nearly two miles before it began to give way, slipping back, widening like the large end of a funnel. Above the sheer walls of the canyon, he could see Foggy Peak off to his right. The ground rose under him sharply into a stand of trees that thinned as the walls opened. Along his left side was a deep fold of a hill against the wall of the canyon. Beyond the trees, he could see the cut clearly now.

On the rim, Chambers saw the figure charge up over the rise, running through the trees.

"Goddamnit," he rasped frantically. McCord was getting away. The bastard was getting away again.

Dismounting hurriedly, the deputy slipped, falling to one knee. Scrambling back up, he jerked the 30.06 from its boot. Working the bolt, he clambered to the canyon rim and, bringing up the rifle, fired quickly.

The trunk of the pine exploded head-high, blasting splinters of wood across Dave's face, and he only half heard the shot crash as his horse reared under him.

Fighting to stay in the saddle, Dave leaned forward as another shot geysered the snow in front of him. The sound of the two shots overlapped each other, rattling through the trees.

Tearing his horse around, heading back down the canyon, Dave heard a third shot, and the sound of them seemed to hover around him as if they had been trapped in the white-covered branches of the pines. Riding, he spotted the drop to one side of him and, pushing his sorrel, he topped the rise and went down it, getting the slope between him and whoever was shooting at him.

Seth had just caught up to Nate and Tom Quade's horse when he heard the two punctures in the silence.

"Damn," he growled. Strapping Nate hard, he ran, leading Tom's horse. Skirting along the sheep, he raced back to the spot where McCord had escaped.

Quade was waiting for him.

Seth came in alongside him, and the sheriff climbed into the saddle like a man twenty pounds lighter and ten years younger.

"I heard 'em, too," the sheriff said, nodding.

"How 'bout Asa and Annie?"

"Looking for their pack animals," Tom said, spurring his horse. "Let's go."

Reining in at the foot of the drop, Dave sat for a moment, trembling.

"Jesus," he murmured, closing his eyes tightly. Then, opening them again, he looked back over his shoulder. "Fool," he spat, angry with himself. He had forgotten about the deputy.

"Trying to kill me," he said, swallowing amazedly. "Bastard is trying to kill me."

Shivering, he tried to think and knew he didn't have time for that.

Dismounting, he scrambled up the slope, sinking to his knees as he approached the top. Lying down flat, he peered over the crest.

The sun went behind a cloud and false darkness ebbed through the white webs of pine. Dark crystal.

His eyes skimmed through the trees, across the head of the canyon to the cliff and up the wall on the other side.

Dave's stomach twisted. Where the hell is he? he wondered, suddenly aching with the cold, and shuddering. He wanted to vomit and urinate at the same time.

His hand gathered a fist of snow and his eyes combed the wall and trees again.

Nothing.

"Damn," he whispered, then growled. "Goddamnit." He looked back down at the sorrel. There was only one way to find out. Slide-running back down the slope, and mounting the horse, he lifted his eyes up the hill. Sweat moistened his lips and armpits.

"Maybe I am crazy," he said with a sigh. Frowning, he spurred the horse.

"Now," he barked.

Bolting, the sorrel pulled up the slope, dragging the crest under him, pounding into the open. Ten feet out, Dave wheeled suddenly, plunging deeper into the trees and down the canyon mouth.

At the crack of the shot he twisted, looking in the direction of the sound to the far wall. Another shot thumped wood. Turning forward in the saddle, Dave saw a snow-laden pine branch rushing toward him. Ducking sidewise, his shoulder smashed through the end of the branch and, screaming, he was ripped backward. Grasping the saddle horn desperately, he stayed in the saddle, hauling himself back up.

The sorrel ran down into the cover of the canyon and Dave managed to stop him. Dave's breath raked through him with jagged edges. Rubbing his shoulder, he worked his arm in its socket. Just bruised, he concluded quickly. Gathering his breath, he looked up the canyon to the far wall.

He was somewhere on that rim, Dave thought, nodding. If he could make it across the flat to the cliff beneath the deputy, he might have enough cover to make it to the cut. As steep as that wall was, the deputy would have a hard time trying to hit anything down there.

At least that's what Dave had to bet on.

He looked down at his hands. They were trembling. Lifting his eyes, he frowned. "Let's get to it," he whispered. Grasping the reins hard, he spurred the sorrel out, giving the horse his head. Pushing him up the rise and into the trees. Back toward the cut. Running.

Two shots rattled through the pines and, threading the trees, Dave hammered toward the foot of the cliff.

Two more quick shots ripped by him.

Swinging through the trees, he could see the cliff wall now. A hundred yards.

He broke from the line of trees into the open.

A flurry of shots geysered the snow around him in a white holocaust blending with the crash of explosions of the walls.

He was closing on the cliff. Fifty yards.

The shots screamed by him.

Twenty—

Something pounded through his hip, ramming him back, tearing him out of the saddle and down into colorless silence, the pain-congealing darkness around him flooding him down . . .

Then thrusting him back.

He was in the snow. Lying on his stomach. Blood scrawled in the white beside him, his hip throbbing painfully.

Blinking snow from his eyes and raising his head, Dave could see his horse trotting away along the foot of the cliff, then stopping.

Dave started to move, then remembered the deputy. He looked to the horse. Too far. The base of the cliff was closer. Fifteen yards or so. If he could make it to the bottom of the cliff, he might have enough cover to make it to the horse.

He tested his leg gingerly to see if it would move. It felt like it was made of memory and lead. But he could use it. Shoving himself up, he crawl-ran, dragging himself toward the cliff base.

Above him, Milt Chambers had stood up when Dave went down. Smiling, he started down the slope, slipping a little and catching himself with his free hand.

"Damn," he muttered. Bringing his eyes up, he saw McCord below him. Up and running.

Forgetting the slope, Chambers brought the rifle up, firing. A plume of snow jerked behind McCord. Swearing, Chambers jerked the bolt out and back, stepping toward the rim to get a better shot.

His foot dropped through the crust.

Fumbling the rifle, he pitched sideways, landing on his butt, sliding down.

"Ahh," he complained, embarrassed. Trying to better his hold on the rifle, he slipped again. Slamming down on his back. Sliding.

"Oh my—"

Still holding on to the rifle, he reached back with his free hand, trying to stop himself. With the rifle in his hand, he careened through the snow and, screaming, plummeted over the rim. . . .

Dave heard the scream and, crouching against the cliff, saw the man and his rifle fall. For a moment it was like a blurred photograph. The man hovered. Pinned in the air like a misshapen butterfly. Then he dropped. Slamming into the cliff wall twenty feet down, he rolled into a cluster of rocks. The rifle which had been flung out landed at the bottom of the cliff, standing straight up in the snow not far from Dave.

Limping to the rifle, Dave picked it up, then lifted his eyes to the deputy. He could see him like a broken doll against the rocks.

Starting up the cliff toward him, Dave heard the echo of hooves back down the canyon.

Seth and Quade. He frowned. He looked at the deputy, then back down at his horse, and shook his head. Using the rifle butt as a crutch, he made his way back down to his horse. Mounting painfully, he turned him toward the cut.

NINE

Lifting Chambers gently, Tom Quade turned him over and, kneeling beside him, felt the pulse in his throat.

He nodded thankfully. "He's alive," he called back down to Seth at the bottom of the cliff.

A shudder of relief jerked through the old rancher. Taking a rope from his saddle, he had started up the slope when he saw the blood on the ground.

"McCord's hit," he called to Quade.

"Worry about that later," the sheriff said.

Climbing the steep incline, he made it to the sheriff and his deputy. They pulled Chambers into a sitting position, then the sheriff and the old man silently slipped the rope around his chest. Then, stringing the rope around a rock, Quade held it, easing out length as Seth maneuvered the deputy down the slope.

Quade followed after Seth and Chambers had reached the bottom. At the foot of the cliff, Seth was looking over the ground. Shaking his head, he turned to help the sheriff with Milt.

"What is it?" Quade asked.

"Milt's rifle," Seth said. "I don't see it anywhere."

Standing, Quade combed the ground with his eyes, and finally frowned deeply.

"Maybe it's still up top."

Seth nodded doubtfully. "Yeah."

"We can look later," Quade said, moving his eyes to the deputy. "Shouldn'ta let him come up here," he said tightly. "If I hadn't been so goddamn softhearted . . ."

"You can be mad at yourself later," Seth said. "Right now we need to get him up to Asa's cabin."

Turning from the night-darkened window, Seth looked at the deputy on the bed across the big main room of Asa's house. He was still unconscious. Quade sat beside him.

At the stove Ann was quietly preparing dinner. She hadn't said anything since the escape that afternoon. A couple of times the old rancher thought Tom was going to say something to her, but his anger had kept him from it. Seth knew the sheriff was trying to calm himself, so when he did talk to her there would be no personal involvement in it.

The door pushed open suddenly and Asa came inside, shaking the snow from his hat and coat.

"Cold as ice," he grumbled. Then, looking to Quade and Chambers, he lowered his voice. "Sorry," he said. Crossing to the stove, he poured himself a cup of coffee.

Seth looked back to the night. Clouds masked the stars and the absolute darkness chilled the old rancher's stomach.

No wonder folks worship light so much, he thought.

Asa sat down at the table and unbuttoned his coat. Quade got up from Chambers' bedside and crossed the wide room to Seth.

"You'll have to go it alone from here," he said.

Seth frowned. "You takin' Milt back?" He gestured to the deputy.

The sheriff nodded. "Got to get him to a hospital. Asa can't do it. Once he got out he might never get back up here. And Annie can't either." He shook his head. "It's got to be me. You know the country. I'd be lost in ten minutes."

Seth's frown deepened and he was quiet for a moment.

"You ain't givin' it up, are you, Seth?"

The old man shook his head. "No," he said. "I ain't givin' it up."

"Dinner," Asa said from the table.

The two men crossed the room and sat down. Turning from

the stove, Ann put the food on the table, then looked to Tom Quade.

"I guess I owe all of you an apology," she said. "Mostly you, Sheriff."

Quade's mouth hardened. "We'll talk about it later," he said.

"Are you going to take me to jail?"

The sheriff stared up at her. "No," he finally answered. "But I sure as hell ought to. What got into you, anyhow?"

Ann's eyes fell. "I don't know," she began, and drew in her breath. "I saw him . . . and I just had to help him. I didn't even think about it. I just started yelling."

"Yeah." Quade frowned.

Ann started to turn back to the stove, then leveled her eyes at the sheriff. "I'm sorry about what I did to you," she said. "But I'm not sorry about helping him. I'd do it again. He's got a right to his chance."

Quade's mouth hardened, and without saying anything he started his meal.

Seth looked up at the girl. "Maybe he has," he said, nodding. "I just wonder if he knows what he's buyin'. . . ."

TEN

Alone, Dave McCord rode down the long mountains into the darkness.

The bullet track across his hip throbbed and the blood had frozen his pants to his leg.

Angling the sorrel down between a fold in the hills and into the beginnings of a stand of pine, he pulled the rifle from its boot and dismounted carefully.

Squinting in the blackness, he spotted a downed trunk off through the brush and, leading the horse and using the butt end of the rifle again, he limped to it.

He sat down on the log, trembling, his breath coming hard, and he could feel his pants leg wetting slightly. The wound was bleeding again.

Time for that later, he thought, frowning, right now he had other things to do.

Taking down the food sack from his horse, he looked through it, then his saddlebags, and sat back wearily. There was no ax or knife. Seth or Quade had taken them out.

Standing and using the rifle as a crutch again, he limped into the trees. He found a few scraps of dead limbs in the pines and carried them back to the trunk.

Scraping out a place in the snow against the trunk, he built a small fire, hobbled his horse, and sat down to look at his wound.

In the light of the fire he undid his pants, and, letting the heat of the flames work on the frozen blood, he pulled out a wad of shirt he had stuffed on the wound.

The bullet had ripped the flesh high on his hip, but missed the bone.

"Lucky," he grumbled ironically, smiling a frown and shaking his head. "Oh well, my butt wasn't my best feature anyway."

The bark of a wolf jerked his eyes up, the sound chilling him. Night moved in the trees.

He eased his eyes back to the wound. No reason that sound should bother him now. He'd heard wolves before. Concentrating on the wound, he took alcohol he'd bought at the store from his saddlebags and, wetting another torn piece of shirt with it, began washing out the wound. The suddenness of the alcohol lanced new pain through him, and he had to rest for a minute.

"Didn't think it could hurt much more," he said, breathing hard. Blinking sweat from his eyes, he sat up again and finished the job. Taking a clean shirt from his bag, he began tearing off the bottom for bandages.

The wolf cried again and he jerked, pulling the wound.

"Damnit," he growled, and slumped against the leg.

An answering cry came from the other direction and Dave felt his bowels tighten.

He wondered for a moment how far away they were, then tried to push the thought from his mind. Nothing to worry about, he nodded, just a touch of Asa's fever. . . .

He looked at the fire and wished he'd brought more wood. He wanted the biggest fire in the world right now. Anything to push back the darkness.

Standing, he went to his horse, unhitched the saddle, and pulled it down. He spread the blanket over the horse, then, sitting down, unrolled his sleeping bag.

It wasn't until he was in the bag and resting back against the saddle that he looked at the food sack and remembered he hadn't eaten. He should eat, he knew that, but he wasn't hungry.

"Tomorrow," he murmured, a sudden weariness dragging him back into the cradle of the saddle.

Staring at the remnants of the fire, he drifted back, and like movement across lightning, he seemed to exist many places at once.

With Heck in the mountains. "Don't belong there no more. . . ."

Then the hospital.

Annie Rule scattering the horses as he ran. Thank you, Annie. Thank—

Annie looking up at him, the dead sheep behind her. "Out here what's weak, sick, or wounded, dies."

A wolf cried, jerking him back to the night and the pain of his wound, and he realized why the sound bothered him now.

"Out here what's weak, sick, or wounded, dies," Annie had said.

His hand touched his wound and his eyes slipped to the dark trees.

"I'll make it," he growled, reaching out for the rifle, pulling it to him. "I'll make it."

Ann Rule twisted beneath her heavy blankets, trying again to fall asleep, but it was no use.

"Damn," she whispered irritably and, pushing aside the blankets, she sat up. She slipped into her houseshoes and robe, glanced restlessly over the room, then padded quietly across the floor. Easing open the door, she went into the main room of the house. In the darkness she could hear the ragged breathing of the deputy, and on the floor, the regular, measured whisper of the sheriff and Seth in their bedrolls. Tiptoeing, she went to the stove. It was still warm and on it was half a pot of coffee left from dinner.

Taking a cup from the shelf, she poured a small amount and tasted it. It was only a little warmer than tepid, but drinkable. She filled the cup, then walked back to her room and closed the door behind her. Sitting down in a chair by her bedroom window, she raised her eyes to the darkness beyond the glass. Hovering. Nearly touching her.

Pulling her eyes down, she looked at the coffee and sipped it.

The rattling of her doorknob drew her gaze around. Her father slipped quietly into the room.

"Heard you up," the old sheepherder whispered, crossing to her, sitting down on the edge of her bed.

"Trouble falling asleep," she explained.

"Yeah," the old man nodded, "me too."

"Coffee in there," she said, holding up her cup.

"That ain't gonna help me sleep, I'm afraid."

"No." Ann tried to smile. "I guess not. Silly," she said, and put the cup down on the floor. "Seem to be doing a lot of silly things lately."

"Like this afternoon?"

She turned in the chair. "I . . . I did do the right thing, didn't I, Papa?"

"What do you think?"

Her eyes glistened with certainty. "Like I told Mr. Quade, I'd do it again."

"Then that's your answer," her father said. "No need to ask me."

She shifted in the chair, looking back out the window. "Then why can't I get it out of my mind? It's over. Done with . . ."

Asa swallowed with difficulty, staring at his daughter. "No," he cut in, "it's not, Annie. Back there this afternoon you made a decision and it ain't finished yet."

"But Dave is gone."

"I'm not talkin' about him," Asa said. "You . . . started somethin' else out there." The next words came hard. "You've started to leave home, Annie. . . ."

Ann shook her head, her breath thickening in her throat. "No, Papa," she protested.

"Listen to me," her father almost growled, a near anger straining his voice. Then he touched her hand. "Annie," he whispered softly, searching for the words, "Annie, folks have to go their own way. Your mama had to. I have to. You do too."

"No," Ann exploded, coming out of the chair and into her father's arms. "Papa, I love you."

"I know that, honey." Asa's arms tightened around her. "I know that. But you have to finish what you've started." He pushed her away a little to see her face. "Tom'll be headin' down tomorrow. Takin' that deputy. I think you'd better see to goin' with him."

Ann trembled violently. "Papa," she choked, "I don't want to leave. I—"

Holding her, the sheepherder trembled too. "None of us ever do, Annie. It ain't easy," he breathed, "it ain't never easy." Still holding her, he talked to her for a long time, trying to explain it to her.

And to himself.

ELEVEN

Gray dawn brushed the air as Seth Mattick shoved his Henry into its boot and turned back to Tom Quade.

"Good luck," the sheriff said.

"I'll need it." Seth nodded and, looking up at the cloud-covered sky, shook his head. "Another damn front," he grumbled.

"Maybe it'll break," Tom said hopefully.

"Yeah." Seth smiled skeptically. "Maybe. Keep an eye out for us."

"How long to Grass River?"

"Three days, with luck. Better call it four."

"How 'bout comin' back this way?"

Seth shook his head, pointing toward the cut through the mountains. "Once another good snow flies, that pass'll fill up with snow. Like a sink in there." He lifted himself into the saddle and Asa came out of the house and down the hill.

"Leavin', I take it?"

"My reputation's at stake." Seth smiled. "Associating with a sheepherder."

"And mine." Asa grinned. "Hear you never can get the smell of a cowman off you."

The two men laughed, then Asa's smile faded into concern. "You really goin' after him?"

"Looks that way."

Asa shook his head. "Sometimes I wonder if you got sense enough to drive nails in a snowbank, Seth. One fool out there's enough."

"You'd think so, wouldn't you," Seth agreed, and started to turn Nate out.

"Seth," Tom said, stopping him. The sheriff's face was lined, taut with what he was about to say.

"What is it, Tom?"

The sheriff frowned. "If you have to—stop him."

"Tom—" Asa protested.

Seth held out his hand to Asa, his eyes narrowing at Tom. "You talkin' about killin' him?"

"No." The sheriff's eyes fell. "With you doin' the shootin' it won't come to that. One in the leg will do. You're the best I've ever seen."

"You're talkin' like he's a criminal, Tom. You heard his story."

"Goddamnit," the sheriff growled. "I've only got his word for that story."

"I believe him."

Quade frowned. "Faith's a luxury I can't afford. All I've got are the facts. He's broken arrest twice. There's a deputy hurt in there, and we never found Milt's rifle."

"Tom—"

"No, Seth. He's a desperate man. Desperate enough to go up against a man with a gun. A man that desperate might hurt somebody that gets in his way. I don't know if he's crazy, and I don't know about his story. It don't matter. My bein' softhearted has got a deputy hurt. It's not going to happen again. Now if you don't want to go after him, that's up to you."

Seth frowned. "I've got to go after him, you know that."

Sighing, the sheriff shrugged. "Didn't mean to get worked up, but ever' time I look at Milt, I—"

"Now you're bein' a fool, Tom. I've got a feelin' what happened to Milt is his own fault."

"He's still a deputy. Injured in the line of duty," the sheriff said flatly.

"You're the sheriff." Seth shrugged and eased his horse out.

"Seth," the sheriff said.

The old rancher looked back.

"Take care." The sheriff gave up the words difficultly.

Seth smiled. "You too, hoss." He nodded, nudging Nate, pushing him down the valley, through the sheep, then the pines.

From a window in the main room of the house, Ann watched
Seth ride out, then looked to her father and Tom Quade coming
back up the hill. Her throat constricted suddenly, painfully, and
she turned away.

Glancing over the room, she looked for something to do.
Anything. She hurried to the stove and began clearing the skil-
lets and pans with heavy, clumsy movements.

Behind her, she heard the two men come into the house,
stomping snow from their boots.

Pushing a skillet down into a bucket of hot, soapy water, she
began to scrub it vigorously.

Quade took a look at Chambers, then began to gather up his
gear. Asa lingered at the door for a moment, staring at his daughter, then slowly crossed to the stove. Standing beside her, he
took a cup from the shelf and poured himself some coffee.

Ann didn't raise her eyes. She cleaned the skillet, rinsed and
dried it, then hung it on the wall. Picking up another, she shoved
it into the soapy water. Out of the corner of her eye she could see
Asa turning and sitting down at the table.

"That about does it," Quade said behind her. "Guess I'll be
headin' out, too. Mind helpin' me, Asa?"

The sheepherder looked at him. "What? Oh, no." Placing his
cup on the table, he got up.

"Gonna have a helluva time gettin' him back down," the
sheriff sighed, grumbling.

At the stove, Ann scraped harder on the skillet. She could
hear Quade moving toward the door; could feel her father's eyes
on her.

The motion of her hands in the water slowly waned and,
turning, she raised her eyes and looked back over her shoulder.

Quade was lifting his saddle. Her father was carrying supplies, his gaze still on her.

Ann opened her fingers, letting the skillet slide away under
the water.

"Mr. Quade," she said, but he didn't hear her. "Mr. Quade," she said again, forcing a strained volume into her voice.

Quade turned. "Yeah?"

"I . . . I've caused you a lot of trouble."

Quade shrugged. "Forget it."

"But I want to ask a favor of you," she went on.

He straightened. "A favor?"

Ann nodded, pointing to Chambers. "You'll need help with him," she began, then sighed. "Damn," she frowned, and raised her eyes, her voice quavering. "I want to go with you, Mr. Quade."

The sheriff blinked. "You, what?"

"I want to go with you," Ann repeated, her voice gaining strength. "Back down the mountains. Back to Three Medicine."

TWELVE

Dave McCord jerked awake, pain hammering through his hip. Sweat bubbled on his forehead and, leaning back into the saddle, he eased his breath through him, then unzipped the bag and pushed himself up stiffly.

He looked to the fire. The coals were still good.

Getting his legs under him and using the rifle as a crutch again, he managed to find enough dead wood in the lower branches of the pine for another fire.

He started the fire and, putting on the coffee, looked up at the sky.

The clouds were holding. Broken over him, but thick to the north. He looked at his watch. Eight o'clock. He frowned and glanced back in the direction he'd come.

They would be after him now.

Maybe last night.

Today for sure.

He looked at the fire. He didn't feel like eating, and it would take time. But he knew he had to.

He poured coffee and forced himself to eat a whole can of stew. With that done, he broke camp and, picking up his saddle, limped stiffly to the sorrel. Lifting the saddle, he could feel the pain in his hip again, and settling it on the horse's back, he leaned against him, fighting down the pain.

Blinking his eyes and looking up, he saw the flicker of movement in the trees.

His eyes snapped open and, holding to the horse, he tried to catch it again, straining to pick something out of the gray-green-black of blending.

Nothing. Only mist and snow and pine.

It had been so quick that there hadn't even been color to it. Just the movement.

Twisting, he looked back up the hill, then back to the trees.

Seth and Quade couldn't have caught up with him this fast. Even if they had, they would have had him by now. No playing games.

His eyes combed the trees as he finished cinching the saddle, then packed the rest of his gear.

Kicking out the fire, he turned to the sorrel and mounted, looking down through the trees, a leaden hot weight in his stomach making him tremble more than the slash in his hip.

"Just Asa's fever." He tried to smile his tension away, easing the horse through the pines. The great trunks whispered by, closing behind him in the mist. The creak of leather and horse hooves in the snow seemed to be held by the fog and trees.

He reined the sorrel in, listening.

The wind laced the pine snow.

He glanced back and then forward and, seeing nothing, shook his head.

"Fever," he assured himself again, a fear thickening in his stomach, but it did no good.

Quade and Mattick were coming.

But there was something else now, too. Not chasing him. Waiting.

Mid-morning. Seth Mattick came off a ridge and, angling toward the trees, following McCord's tracks, spotted the log and the remains of the fire.

And something else.

Kneeling, he touched the four-toed prints in the snow and stood again, looking through the trees.

"Wolves," he whispered.

Dave reined in his horse and looked up at the canyon wall standing in front of him.

Shaking his head, he sighed a laugh. "Rode into a box . . ."

Pulling the sorrel around, he started back down the canyon, keeping his eyes on the walls, looking for a break of some kind.

An hour later he saw his chance. The walls of the canyon had eased to about a thirty-degree angle, and in the snow, Dave could make out a cut running up the face of the wall, wide at the bottom, narrowing toward the top.

Leaning forward in the saddle, he frowned deeply. It was either here or double back and lose more time. His eyes went up the wall again. It looked to be mostly dirt and shale. Fair footing for the sorrel.

"Some days," he said, sighing.

The sorrel shifted his weight, snorting.

He measured the cut again. Fifty feet maybe.

"Hell," he growled, and nudged the horse to the wall.

The horse backstepped at first, then, with Dave prodding him harder, he took the shale and dirt, pulling at it hard, his hooves reaching.

"Let's go," Dave said gently, trying to soothe the animal with his voice.

The horse pumped with his back legs and, clawing with his front, struggled to bring the rim of the canyon near. He tried to swerve out to one side and Dave tightened the leather to keep him in line, then slacked it when he took more of the wall.

Keeping his weight forward, Dave kept talking to the sorrel, mostly muttering, hoping the false confidence of his voice would convince his horse that they could make it.

The horse reached again. And again. Loose snow and shale clattered down the slope, the cut narrowing under them.

Reaching again, the sorrel hit solid rock, his hoof slipping. He slumped hard to the left, pitching Dave forward, slamming his shoulder into the horse's neck. Clutching the mane, he kept from coming out of the saddle, and twisting his hip, he felt the wound tear slightly.

"Damn," he moaned, and halted the horse. He was fifteen or

twenty feet from the rim. Trembling, he looked back down the slope, then at the horse.

"Not much of a choice." He frowned, then, strapping the sorrel, he whooped, giving the horse his head. The animal bolted, pawing his way up the slope, hammering across the rock, and stretching, making the rim, then over it, and Dave hauled him in.

Dismounting carefully, Dave opened his coat and touched the wet spot where the blood had come through. Not much, he judged, and, unhitching his pants, he tore another piece from his shirt and put it over the bandage.

He buckled his pants and leaned against the saddle, looking ahead. A ridgeline and several hills fell into a valley and a stand of pines.

"Damn." He sighed wearily. He was tired. All he really wanted—

A speck of movement on the ridgeline to the south jerked up his eyes.

His hands tightened on the saddle horn.

It was a rider.

"Damnit," he growled, lifting his foot to the stirrup, pulling himself stiffly back into the saddle. He watched the rider for another minute. Dark. Hovering against the whiteness. A mile away, maybe two.

That blind canyon—one mistake—had cost him.

The horse shifted under him and, glancing down, he touched the stock of the rifle in its boot.

His jaw hardened and he spurred the sorrel hard, running him.

Seth came slowly along the ridge. He had seen McCord come out of the box canyon, stop for a time, then run for the cover of the wooded valley. The old man halted, watching the fugitive until he blended into the pines.

A tired smile soured his face.

"Don't make it easy for me, son," he sighed.

It took him an hour to cover the distance to a rise above the valley. His eyes studied the pines and, seeing nothing, he moved out again above the treeline.

Below him, the valley lifted, piling into a long swell of hills, a chain of peaks rising beyond them. As the pines began to thin, Seth reined in to examine the ground.

No tracks came out. At least not north.

Frowning, Seth eased around and backtracked halfway down the valley.

Dismounting, he hunkered down, scanning the ground.

The quiet ate into his bowels. The pines stood immobile, a breath of wind the only movement.

"Damn," he spat and, mounting again, he rode back to the head of the valley, down the long slope to Dave's scattering of tracks leading into the trees.

The tree trunks began to slip by him and the old man shifted uneasily in the saddle.

He glanced down at his Henry, but left it there. There was a good chance Dave had Milt's 30.06. He just hoped he was right about that young fella. . . .

The tracks snaked deeper into the trees, winding, coming back on themselves, then going on straight.

Makin' me follow, the old man grimaced. Makin' me kill time.

Or ride into a trap.

The cold seemed to press through his mackinaw suddenly, bleeding into his bones. It had been a long time since he had been afraid.

"Take it easy, Dave," he said aloud, and wondered just what the hell he was doing out here.

Nate stepped out beneath him, pulling them through the pines, down a small hill, and into a draw. Slowing the dun, Seth looked back around. The tracks slipped into the draw.

Seth headed Nate up the side and along the rim of the cut, following the tracks from above. Around the first bend they slashed up the opposite side, over a small grade, and were gone.

Seth sat for a long moment, considering it. "Damned if I do, and damned if I don't." He sighed wearily and, nudging his dun, they eased down the side of the draw and up the other side.

He topped the grade, the uneasiness in his bowels tautening.

He rode down the slope, skirting a steep hill to the north, then into a gorge between the hills. Coming around a spray of boulder, he saw the sorrel standing riderless in front of him.

The old man's first instinct was to turn.

"Right there," McCord's voice said from behind him in the boulders. "Keep facing front."

The tautness in Seth's bowels pulsed fishhooks and, forcing a smile, he shook his head. "You're wastin' time if you're gonna shoot me, son."

"Not what I had in mind," he heard Dave say. Then the sound of his boots in the snow came toward him. "Get down," he quietly ordered the old man.

Seth stayed in the saddle.

"I'm not in the mood." Dave's voice hardened. "I've got this rifle on you and I don't want to hurt you. But don't push it."

Shrugging, the old man slipped his foot from the stirrup and, stepping down, turned to face Dave. The fugitive limped up to him, the rifle leveled at the old rancher's stomach.

"What now?" Seth asked.

"You walk for a while," Dave replied. "I'm takin' your horse. He'll be three hours up the way. Which means you'll have to do a little walking after nightfall to get to him."

"I'll just come after you again."

Dave nodded. "I know, but you won't have a rifle. That'll be in Grass River."

Keeping the 30.06 on Seth, he limped around the old rancher and took Nate's reins.

Seth pointed to McCord's hip. "That where Milt got you?"

Dave nodded. "Nice fella, that deputy. Tried to kill me." His face darkened. "How is he?"

Seth shrugged. "Alive. Barely." His eyes narrowed questioningly. "He didn't give you no chance to surrender?"

"Not unless it woulda been with a bullet through my head."

"Come back and tell it that way."

Dave shook his head. "This really tears it for me. Now if it's not the hospital, it'll sure as hell be jail."

"That's true enough," Seth allowed, then looked at the wound again. He could see the blood on Dave's pants. "How bad is it?"

Dave glanced down at it, then shrugged. "Bleeding some. I'll be all right."

Seth's lips pressed in a frown. "You're not gonna make it."

Dave grinned. "I'll make it," he said, backing toward his sorrel. "You'll have a helluva time catching me, and a harder time stopping me without a gun, because that's the only way you're gonna do it."

Seth shook his head. "Not talking about me, son. You know you got wolves on your track?"

Dave hesitated, blinking, remembering the movement in the trees that morning. Then, pushing a smile through his lips, he shook his head. "Won't do any good, Seth, tryin' to scare me. That's a wives' tale about wolves attacking men."

"Is it?" the old man snapped. "I'll bet you read that someplace. Damnit, get it through your head it's different out here."

"No use, Seth."

"Listen." Seth gentled his voice. "You're right, wolves won't hit an upright man or a man on a horse. But on foot and bleeding you're just another wounded animal. You lose that horse and they'll kill you."

Still backing, Dave reached his horse. "I'm not goin' back. I'm gonna make it to those trees, Seth."

"Even if it means goin' over me?"

"If it comes to it," Dave said quietly.

"Survival at any cost."

"That's the way it is with all of us. I'm just beginning to learn it."

"You sound like your father now."

"Maybe there are some good things to be learned from him." The young man's eyes narrowed. "What is it anyway, Seth?

What're you doin' out here? You said your place—" He stopped and nodded. "The reward. That's what keeps you comin', isn't it?"

Seth stared at him but didn't answer.

· "Survival." Dave nodded. "You or me. One of us has to lose for the other to win."

Keeping the rifle on the old man, Dave clumsily mounted the sorrel.

"See you, son," Seth said.

"Maybe not." The fugitive nodded. "Maybe I can outrun you yet." He frowned regretfully. "If I can't, I guess it'll come down to you or me."

Turning the horses out, and leading Nate, he ran down the gorge.

THIRTEEN

McCord slipped behind the shoulder of the hill and Seth was alone.

You or me, McCord, he thought, nodding. You or me.

He started walking first, then jogged out at a slow, steady pull. Back down the gorge, around the hill, dragging his feet through the white, trying not to think about it, trying not to think about anything except moving his legs.

He stopped above the creekbed, carefully easing the cold air through him.

McCord had turned back down his own tracks, skirting the steep, rugged hill to the north. Seth looked to the slope, studying it. One hundred and fifty yards up it. Hard angle. Damn near straight up at the top.

Heading north, McCord would come back around it.

Frowning, Seth climbed the rim of the draw and started up the slope. He just might be able to save most of those three hours. The grade began to pull up in front of him and he could feel it in his chest, his breath grinding raw, cutting into his lungs, thickening into a weight in his chest. He kept moving at a steady pace, centering his concentration on it. He pushed Dave from his mind, the ranch, the money, everything, focusing on the slope and each step he took, his eyes slipping up and over the ground, picking the most level ground, avoiding any sinks of snow.

The slope steepened and the old man's breath began to come harder, dragging through him. He had to use the trunks of the trees now, pulling himself up, then pushing on to the next one, pulling again. The aspen and pine began to scatter into the rocks and he stopped, kneeling down, regulating his breathing again, concentrating on getting the pain out of his chest.

Standing, he looked up.

The last twenty feet of the slope jutted up in front of him.

Not bad, he thought, breathing hard. Striding out, he started up the incline.

The rocks beneath him began to thrust up. Getting down on his hands and knees, the old rancher was crawling now, scrambling his way up the rocks.

The top was close now.

Hurrying, his boot slipped over a snow-covered rock and his knee cracked into it.

"Goddamnit," he barked, and, getting his other leg under him, he kept moving. He couldn't stop now. A thick layer of sweat was chilly on his face and matted his back, arms, and chest. He put weight on the knee and it held. Climbing. Around a scrub pine. Crawling. Pulling himself up.

He hauled himself over the top and sat down.

He felt the knee he'd hit. No blood, just a good scrape, he concluded, and, looking down the slope, he could see the hills to the north and part of the valley. Edging down the crest, he was able to see more of the valley. Combing the pines, the old man sat down. It took him a minute to spot McCord. His red pile-lined coat flickered in the green-white. Coming around the slope below the old man. Headed north.

Reeling, the old man stumbled along the crest twisting out toward the hills. As the crest began to spread away, Seth dropped down the slope. Skirting the trees, he stayed above the treeline, running north.

Up the valley he could see McCord coming out of the forest, pulling toward the hills; then he was gone, swallowed by the folds of earth.

Seth trotted along the trees at the north end and, coming out on easier ground, strode out, jogging again. His lungs were lead now, tearing in his chest, his breath hammering in him. He followed McCord's trail to where he had disappeared and, halting, rested for a moment, regulating his breathing.

The old man looked up at the sky, wishing he had the sun to tell time by. He'd never owned a watch. Guessing, he figured an hour or so had passed and he had gained that much time on McCord.

By cutting across what he figured McCord's line of travel to be, he might narrow some more of that time.

Walking again, he eased away from the tracks. He moved up the hills, keeping to the high ground. In the distance, the peaks blended in the fog and snow. A wind, gentle at first, pushed across the hills, brushing Seth's face. A sudden gust slammed into him and it seemed like his coat wasn't even there. Gaining strength, the wind picked up dry snow, making a white, drifting wall in front of him, then just as suddenly the wind was gone and the peaks were clear in front of him again, but the cold was still there, pulsing into him.

He walked, his feet beginning to ache. Boots weren't made for the ground. The soles were thin so that he could feel the stirrups through them, and now he could feel every rock. The high heels made him awkward on the ground. A horseman afoot was the sorriest animal alive.

The more he walked, the madder at McCord he got. Not long now, he thought.

His feet were wet now, the boots soaked through, and he knew that his feet would freeze if he didn't change socks and dry the leather.

"Not long now," he assured himself, and found himself saying it more and more; it was good to hear the sound of his own voice whispering.

He came down a hill and, sitting down, pulled off his boots, peeled away the wet socks and, tearing lengths from his shirt, wrapped his feet and jerked the boots back on. Standing again, the weariness and cold thickened in him, pushing him back, and for a moment he didn't know whether he was going to be able to get up.

"Old," he whispered. He was seventy years old. Seventy years of this country, and chasing men. Funny how he'd probably blown away enough money in that time to keep his place, and now it all depended on one man.

"Damn," he murmured, and thought about sitting there for a long time, building a fire and getting warm. The memory of warmth was like a woman. Soft.

What the hell did it matter? He looked up toward the mountains.

It mattered.

Doing something mattered more than not doing something.

He had to get up and walk. And he had to catch McCord.

Pushing himself up, he started walking again, wading, pulling himself through the snow.

He looked to the mountains.

"You're gettin' awful contrary," he said aloud to them. "Shouldn't be treatin' friends like this."

The peaks shifted color with the movement of the clouds.

Maybe we ain't friends no more, the old man thought, sighing. Maybe we never were.

He'd felt like they were home once. And he felt a stranger now. . . .

He had to concentrate to keep his mind on walking. He found himself thinking about everything but, and slowing down. He couldn't do that. He—

Coming over a small hill, he saw Nate tied to a pine limb in the drop below him.

"Jesus." The old rancher sighed thankfully. "McCord kept his word." Running, he slogged through the snow and pounded into the horse.

Nate looked at him irritably.

"You old bastard," Seth laughed, rubbing the dun's neck, then looked at the rifle boot. The Henry was gone. "Why didn't you bite him or something?" the old man asked.

Nate just stared at him.

"I know," Seth said, nodding. "You forgot."

Mounting, the old rancher looked down at his feet. He should dry his boots and put on some dry socks. But he had gained on McCord and he wasn't going to lose it now.

He pulled Nate around.

"Later," he whispered. "Later."

Nightfall came early, and Seth followed the tracks until the last light was gone, then pushed on, walking again, staying in the tracks by feel. He made himself stop then, knowing he could lose the trail too easily, and maybe the time he'd made up on McCord.

He reined Nate in and made camp. He started his coffee and began to dry out his boots.

He looked into the darkness, trying to pick out any flicker of fire.

Seeing nothing, he turned back to the fire and poured himself some coffee.

"Tomorrow mornin'," he said, nodding. He would have him before noon. Then he could go home.

FOURTEEN

Seth was up before first light. Stirring out of his bedroll, he pulled on his boots and drank coffee from his thermos. The heat bit through him. Finishing the coffee, he rolled up the sleeping gear and fed and saddled Nate.

Night spread away slowly. Drifting apart from itself. Gently mixing with the light as Seth pulled himself into the saddle, turning Nate out and up the hills.

Riding, the mist mingled around him, enveloping and separating with the light, gold now, white, and black. The horse reached out under him, pulling up a slope. Coming up on a crest, Seth looked down into the deep folds of hills, snow-stilled and green. And in front of him the peaks suddenly pushed through the mist and clouds.

The old rancher hesitated for a moment, staring up at them. Then, nudging Nate, he dropped down the crest, angling into the trees. At the bottom of the slope he noticed smaller tracks around McCord's. Leaning out in the saddle, Seth nodded.

Wolves.

Straightening himself, he hoped two things. That those wolves had fed recently and that Dave didn't lose his horse.

He rode hard for another two hours, following McCord's tracks toward the peaks, twisting up a long arroyo. Coming out of it, he saw the fugitive top a small knoll three hundred yards away, then drop from sight.

"Nate," the old man barked, and the dun bolted under him, hooking his hooves into the snow, running.

Seth covered the distance to the knoll. Coming over it, he saw McCord hammering hard down the bottom of the knoll and starting up a long slope, angling around the peaks in front of them and into a stand of rocks, then out of sight again.

Giving Nate his head, Seth followed, slashing up the slope.

The echo of a shot pounded across the snow and Seth jerked the dun in.

Another shot crashed in the roll of the first, but no lead hit near Seth.

"Seth," McCord screamed a warning.

"I hear you," the old man nodded.

"Go back, Seth. I don't want to hurt you."

The old man leaned forward on his saddle horn. "You're no killer, Dave."

Silence.

"Don't push it, Seth."

"That's up to you."

Seth sat for a moment, waiting for an answer. The wind cut across the snow.

"Dave?"

The dun shifted under the old man and, frowning, he nodded. There was no place to go but forward.

"Nate." He sighed and the horse stepped out slowly.

The only thing left of McCord in the rocks were his tracks and two empty shell casings. Dismounting, Seth walked through the boulders and into the open. McCord had cut down a long slope, taking the easy way. Seth pulled his eyes back to the mountains and smiled.

The spine of the peak jutted off north, and by going that way the old man could avoid the slowness of winding through the snow-filled cuts down there.

"You just made another mistake," he whispered.

An hour later the old man spotted Dave emerging from the hills below him, dropping down a saddle between two mountains. Seth brought his eyes forward. The saddle narrowed into a wide hook of trees and boulders above McCord. McCord would have to go through them.

Seth turned down the spine, threading into the hook. Staying high in the pine and aspen, Seth watched the fugitive come into the hook, pushing his sorrel hard. Easing down and out of his saddle, the old man tied Nate to a low bough and, taking his rope, he slipped down into the rocks.

Still above McCord, Seth could see the fugitive's red coat coming from a long way away. Resting back on his haunches, the old man waited.

"Hey!" Dave yelled, and feeling himself being dragged back, his hands closed automatically around the saddle horn and the food sack hanging from it. The rope tauted and under him the sorrel jackknifed backward. The rope went slack, then suddenly tight again. Trying to keep the reins in his hand, McCord jerked the sorrel's head hard. The sorrel jumped, lurching forward, hammering out at the end of the rope, and Dave's hands clawed loose from the saddle horn. He grasped the food sack desperately, tearing it from the horn. Tumbling back out of the saddle, Dave slammed into the snow on the bow of his shoulder, crushing the air from his chest and releasing his grip on the sack.

Above the fugitive, the sorrel crow-hopped, smashing his hooves down into the food sack several times. Gagging to pull air into his lungs, McCord twisted in the snow, rolling, trying to get out from under the horse.

On the shelf, Seth jerked the rope hard, hauling McCord away from the horse, then kept it taut as he started down. McCord cawed for breath and, shoving his knees under him, he pushed to his feet. The rope jerked him down again. Pain from his wound chopped through him, and he stayed down for a moment; then, charging up, he limped toward Seth, slacking the rope before the old man could bring it in. Still on the slope, Seth jumped, hanging the slack around a pine trunk, snapping the rope out, wrenching Dave forward, twisting him down on his back again.

"Dave," he said wearily, but the fugitive was stumbling to his feet, pawing up the slope faster than he could move.

Struggling, Dave closed his hands on the rope and, charging, pummeled into the old man, driving his shoulder into his stomach, ramming both of them down, writhing in the snow.

Reeling, Seth thrust off the younger man. Then, coming up, McCord hit the old man in the neck, hammering him back into the snow. On his knees, Dave started for Seth, but the old man jacked his boot into McCord's wounded hip. Screaming, Dave went down. Seth fumbled to his feet, still off balance when Dave burst up into him, throwing his fist into the old man's stomach. The old man sidestepped, catching only half the blow.

Stumbling, Seth tried to keep his feet, but McCord kept coming.

Young, the old man thought rapidly, young and too quick.

"Damn," he growled. Dropping to his knees, he swung his right elbow, pounding it into Dave's wound.

The leg went out from under the younger man and he toppled through a snow-heavy pine bough. Seth burst up, closing on McCord, driving his fist into his stomach, then downing him with a blow to the jaw.

McCord rustled in the snow, fighting to get up, then his breath thumped out of him and he rested down on his face. He was quiet.

Seth stood over him for a moment; then, kneeling beside McCord, he touched the blood on his pants.

Breathing heavily, the old man shook his head. "Damn," he said, sighing regretfully. "Damn . . ."

FIFTEEN

Dave came to slowly.

He became aware of things like gathering fragments. Movement somewhere. The pain in his hip. The smell of coffee and beans. Cold on his face.

The rest of him was warm. He was under something. His sleeping bag.

Dragging his eyes open, he tried to sit up but his hands wouldn't work right. Blinking, he tugged at his hands again, but they still wouldn't move.

Panic bolted him up and the bag slipped off him. Looking down, he could see the ropes around his wrists.

Jerking his eyes up, he saw Seth kneeling beside a fire.

"You bastard," he growled thickly.

The old man's eyes came around and he smiled slowly.

"Best calm down, son."

"You bastard," he spat again. Struggling against the ropes and the pain in his hip, he tried to get up.

Seth stood suddenly. "Now sit down," he ordered McCord sharply. "Or I'll sit you down."

Trembling, McCord did as he was told and found himself sitting against a tree trunk. Wincing at the pain in his hip, he looked down at it. It had been freshly bandaged.

"Sorry about havin' to do that," Seth said. "Hittin' you there, I mean. But you're a mite younger than I am." The old man's face flushed slightly. "Had to fight a little dirty."

"Lucky you didn't kick me in the crotch," Dave grumbled sourly.

The beginnings of a grin pushed at Seth's mouth. "Tell you

the truth, I didn't think of that," he admitted, and shrugged. "Not as versatile as I used to be. Just take the first thing that comes along."

"Thanks," Dave said, nodding.

"'Sides," Seth winked, "you'da kicked me in the crotch if you'da got the chance. Point was to win, wasn't it?"

A grin forced its way through Dave's anger, and he surrendered to it, shaking his head. "Probably nothin' down there to kick."

"Well," the old man sniffed, "if you get the chance, don't. I ain't aged all over."

Dave grinned openly, then touched his wound. "Jesus, that hurt, Seth."

"My feet didn't feel too good yesterday either."

"Damn lucky I left the horse at all." His eyes narrowed. "How the hell'd you catch up with me, anyway? Thought I had four or five hours on you."

"Cross country. Man on foot can go places a man on horseback can't."

"Yeah." The young man frowned. "Weren't worried about losin' my trail?"

Seth pushed back his hat. "You know where you're headed. And I know. Ain't hard findin' you."

"Forgot that."

"Not a good thing to forget." Seth nodded.

"So I found out." He sighed. "Next time I won't forget."

"Won't be any next time," Seth said.

Dave lifted his eyes, leveling his gaze on the old man. "There'll be a next time, Seth."

Seth shook his head with weary frustration. "You're the damnedest, boy. You know that. Don't do nothin' the easy way. Even picked the hardest goddamn place in the world to get to for a hiding place. Damn . . ." He sighed, then his eyes narrowed and came back to the young man.

"Why up here, son? Why these mountains?"

Dave looked at him slowly. "I don't know." He shrugged. "To be free, I guess . . ."

"Lot of places you can be free."

"No," Dave said. "Not anymore. Not down there. Not the way you can be up here. There's another kind of freedom up here."

The old man's eyes softened as he listened to him. "Heard a lot of men talk that way," he said after a moment. "Men to ride the river with. All of 'em gone now."

Dave shook his head. "The mountains are still here. Some of it's the same as it was when they came across it. Settled some of it."

The old man nodded. "They settled it and left, Dave. Like your father and grandfather. Like my son. Your grandfather said it right. They don't belong up here no more. Once they're gone, I don't know that they can ever come back to it. They're different. Bred a different race. They don't belong to the land no more."

"I don't believe that, Seth," McCord said, and his eyes softened. "What about you . . . ?"

The old man's brows gathered. "What about me?"

"You still belong out here, don't you?"

The old man stared at Dave, then blinked, avoiding his gaze. "Sometimes I wonder, son . . . sometimes I wonder." He cleared his throat and pointed to Dave's hip. "We'll rest today. Nearly nightfall anyhow. Head out in the mornin'."

"Back to Asa's?"

The old man shook his head. "No. That pass at Asa's is likely to be closed. We'll go on to Grass River. Down from these peaks, out across another small chain, about a day and a half from here." He looked up at the clouds and added, "Maybe."

Seth felt the temperature drop like he'd been slapped.

Sitting at the fire dishing up the food he'd prepared, he looked up toward the peaks. They were gone.

Dark clouds rushed down on them, swirling through the pines.

Dave looked up, squinting into the mist. "Feels colder," he said.

Seth frowned. "Yeah." He finished with the plates and turned to Dave, handing him one.

McCord placed the plate on his knees, then, taking a fork from Seth, stabbed at the beans and, tipping the plate, spilled some of the food over his leg. "Damn," he grumbled. Putting down the fork, he tried to pick up the plate, and dumped the rest of the beans.

Putting down his plate, Seth shook his head.

"If I take those ropes off," he pointed, "you give me your word you won't make trouble?"

Dave looked up. "Sure, Seth."

"Your word?"

"My word." He nodded.

Reaching under his coat, Seth brought out his knife. Easing forward, he grasped Dave's hands and cut the rope around one hand.

Dave bolted, exploding up into Seth. The old man caught the blow on his shoulder and, pivoting, the cut rope still in his hand, he swung Dave around, slamming him down into the snow.

Dave struggled to get to his feet but, swinging a kick into his legs, Seth knocked him down again.

The fugitive blinked and looked up at the old man, nodding his surrender. "Who said you weren't fast?"

Kneeling down, Seth pinned Dave's arms up behind him. "Up," he said, and they both got up. Seth backed him to the horses, where he cut another length of rope and tied Dave's hands in front of him again.

"Waste of perfectly good rope," the old man complained. He shoved Dave down against the tree. "You gave me your word," he said, standing back.

Dave frowned regretfully. "I'll do it again. I'm getting there, Seth."

Picking up the spilled plate, Seth went back to the fire and dished up another serving.

"Was a time a man's word was worth something." He brought the plate back to Dave. "I guess that's gone, too." He pointed at the food he'd given to Dave. "Gonna have to make do this time."

Nodding, Dave placed the plate on his legs and, taking a fork, ate without spilling any.

The snow started as Seth was finishing the dishes. Raising his eyes to the sky, he frowned. Suddenly there was a shroud of snow across everything, and the temperature felt like it had dropped again.

"Damn," he said with a sigh.

"What is it?" Dave asked.

"Feels like a norther comin' in."

Dave glanced up and around, nodding in agreement. "What do you think?"

"We could try gettin' through it. Then again, it might let up in a day or so."

"Holin' up might be best. Between the two of us, we've got food enough—"

The old man shook his head. "We ain't got yours no more. Your horse trampled it when I dragged you off him. Mine's it."

A needle of fear touched Dave's stomach. "How long'll it last?"

The old man frowned. "Stretchin' it—five, six, maybe seven days. But that's stretchin' it." He looked down at Dave, and at the wound, then shook his head wearily. "It's all we can do, though. With your hip the way it is, you need the rest. Open it again and you'd be no good in a blizzard." He turned to the gear. "Thing to do now is to find some better cover."

After packing quickly, he pushed Dave up into the saddle and, taking the reins to his prisoner's horse, he mounted Nate.

Leading out, Seth pushed out of the trees and back up toward the spine coming down from the mountains.

"Where do you think?" Dave asked.

Seth pointed up toward the hogback dropping from the peak. "Some tree cover up there," he said, "and that line of rock'll break the snow a little."

Pushing up the slope, the wind buffeted them hard.

"Damn . . ." the old man whispered. Bending into the wind, he kept the horses moving. Looking back around at Dave, Seth saw him glancing around, carefully examining the ground.

"I wouldn't," the old man shouted. "No time to be de-horsin' yourself."

Dave looked up at him and smiled guiltily.

"All of a sudden you're not such bad company. Not as long as you've got my horse."

Turning back around, Seth pushed Nate into the cover of pines. Deeper into the trees, he could see the thrust of the rock spine rising above them like a wall. The old man dismounted, then helped Dave from his horse.

"Sit down," he ordered him.

"Let me help," the tied man shouted back.

Seth stared at him for a long moment, then shook his head. "Can't take a chance. Sit down."

Doing as he was told, Dave turned and sat down next to a tree. Seth took his rope from his saddle and, stringing it tight around the trunk, tied McCord to it. Seth examined the knots; then, winking at his prisoner, he turned and walked to the wall. Finding two pines close together, the old man undid his coat and took out his hunting knife. He walked down the face of the wall until he came to a small aspen. Kneeling down, he hacked through it with his knife, then found another and cut it down, too. He dragged the two saplings back to the pines he'd chosen and tied each of them to one of the pines with spare cord from his saddlebags, then pulled them back at a forty-five-degree angle from the pines. He cut two stakes from low pine branches, then went to the ends of the aspens and started driving in the stakes. The ground was hard. Not completely frozen, but hard nonetheless. Using the butt end of his knife, he beat the stakes into the ground, pounding them in slowly, the motion dragging through him, seeming endless and futile. But finally they went in, and he slumped back.

Resting for a moment, Seth's eyes moved through the trees, picking out more low branches. The old man struggled to his feet again and, hacking at the branches, cut them from the trees and piled them behind him. When the pile was waist high, he pulled them, two at a time, back to the aspen poles and stacked them on, lapping them over each other until they covered the poles, making a roof and enough room to lie down beneath. Pushing back to the trees, he cut more limbs and stacked them along at the sides. Finished, he waded back to Dave and untied him, then, leading the horses, slogged back to the lean-to.

Seth tied the horses as near to the wall as he could, fed them a little oats, then both men fell into the lean-to, exhausted.

What seemed to be a long time later, Dave opened his eyes and sat up. His eyes roamed over the makeshift shelter.

"Think it'll hold?" he asked, his breath still coming hard.

Seth pushed himself up. "Think so," he wheezed. "Not much wind down here. At least we're out of that."

Dave pointed up, moving his finger between the two pines. "Might put a crossbar there, put somethin' heavy up and down across the back, then tie it. That'll hold it some."

Seth nodded. "Good idea. Ain't finished, anyway. Got to rig a reflector, too."

The old man pulled himself up and gestured to the tree behind Dave. "Sit down a bit."

Dave frowned. "Seth, I won't—"

"We've been through that, remember?"

"Goddamnit," the fugitive snapped. "I give you my—" Hesitating, he sighed. "I know." He nodded. "We've been through that. Damn," he grumbled, and sat back against the pine, and Seth tied him to it.

"Don't know where the hell I'd go," he offered, watching Seth.

Fixing the last knot, Seth stepped back, a smile tugging his lips. "You'd think of something," he assured him.

The old man peered to the snow. It was falling harder now. There was still no wind. At least not down here. Pulling up his collar, and slipping his knife from his coat again, the old rancher pushed back into the open.

The old man worked methodically. Cutting another aspen. Tying it between the pines. Finding four small pines, cutting them down, then piling them lengthwise on the lean-to for weight. His old muscles ached with fatigue and cold, but he knew he had to keep moving. Night was in the snow.

He tied down the heavier pine limbs, then went back to the trees and cut green limbs. Just under the front of the lean-to he fought the hard ground again and pounded half-inch-thick sticks into the ground in pairs and in a straight line three feet long. The pairs of sticks were half an inch apart; between them, Seth rested more green sticks, stacking them on top of each other. He built the reflector until it covered the front of the lean-to and stood three feet high. He scooped out the snow and, finding rocks, built a small hearth, between the lean-to and the reflector.

It took him another hour to gather firewood, scouring through the lower boughs for dead branches; then, finding a downed trunk, he set to work again with his knife. Sweat mopped through his underwear to his shirt, and his muscles began to feel like the wood he was cutting. Night pressed through the falling snow, ebbing the pines, but the old man kept working, hauling the wood, stacking it inside, then going back for more, his movements mechanical, his weariness and the darkness blending, whispering an echo back at him. A silent pulse shared by the old man and the night—a song of rest—angered him and he pushed on, forcing himself to work.

Dave watched guiltily as the old man worked. Then, as he began stacking the wood inside, the fugitive shoved his legs around, scraping the snow out of the lean-to, slowly working down to the ground.

Seth trudged back through the snow, nearly falling as he piled the wood into the hearth. His eyes jerked over the cleared area and he vaguely nodded approval to Dave, then went to work on the fire.

"Last of it until tomorrow." The old man coughed, and with trembling hands he started the fire and sat back.

"That green wood," he whispered. "It'll keep most of the heat back in here. Best not to have the fire too high."

Dave nodded. A silence hovered between them as they watched the snow fall.

After a long moment, the old man sighed disgustedly. "Jesus," he mused. "Keeps comin' down like that we'll be able to make ourselves some snowshoes and walk over the tops of the Leyendas."

Seth cooked a can of stew for dinner and split it between them.

"Don't spill that," he said, handing Dave his plate, sitting down next to him. "We're gonna have to make do."

Dave started to take a bite, then hesitated, watching the old man. "Seth," he frowned, "I know you're hungrier than that."

"It'll do." The old man inclined his head in assurance.

"No need to starve ourselves. We've got plenty to make it to Grass Valley."

"Maybe." The old man nodded. "Maybe not. Preserve what you got till you get more."

"All right." Dave sighed. "Then take this," he said, holding out his plate. "You've been doin' all the work."

Seth smiled back at him. "Don't worry, son, I ain't gonna die. I ain't ready."

The prisoner reflected his grin. "You're a hard-to-get-along-with bastard."

"That's how I got to be seventy." The old man nodded.

Dave ate reluctantly, and when he was finished Seth scraped both plates out with snow. Setting the plates down by the fire, Seth filled a small pot with snow, set it by the fire, and filled it with dry beans.

"Hope you like beans. They'll be soaked by tomorrow."

Dave nodded and Seth settled back, pushing his Henry and Milt's 30.06 to the side away from Dave.

The prisoner nodded at the old man's rifle.

"That a Henry?"

Seth grinned. "Probably made by B. Tyler himself."

Dave's eyes narrowed questioningly and, understanding, Seth continued. "B. Tyler Henry. Fella that more or less invented it.

Along with Winchester. Grandpappy got that in the Civil War. 'Bout the only thing he did get."

"Still any good?"

Seth eyed his prisoner for a moment and then nodded. "At three hundred yards I can drop anything with it, if that's what you're wantin' to know."

Dave gave up a laugh. "That's what I wanted to know," he admitted.

The old man smiled, too. "You're about as subtle at this as a horse hatchin' an egg."

The young man's mouth shadowed slightly. "Afraid I haven't been at this long." He stretched back against the tree, trying to get comfortable with his hands bound. He looked back to Seth.

"Your place," he began slowly. "You in pretty bad trouble?"

"Bad enough," the old man said. "Lost a lot of stock this summer. Didn't make the money to buy feed for the calves in the spring, or to get their mothers through the winter."

"What would happen then?"

"In another year I'd lose the place," the old man said. "But that ain't gonna happen. I ain't gonna lose that ranch."

Seth pushed two more logs into the fire and, nodding, settled back into his blankets. He looked to Dave, twisting over his side in his sleeping bag, trying to adjust his bound hands.

The old man moved his eyes to the night and falling snow. Cold laced into the lean-to, but the reflector pushed back more heat onto them than he remembered. The flames curled around the new wood, seeping light up and over the reflector into the pines shadowing them, flickering them like old film, breathing memories into the old man, shadows themselves. Ella. And the boys. Harve. An engineer, a maker of rockets and aircraft in California. A father, himself, of a boy and a girl. Children now grown, that Seth had hardly ever seen. At first Harve had come back every year, then less often. The children had Seth's blood in them, but they were people he didn't know. Harve had loved the mountains, too, Seth remembered, but somehow things began to come up, and he seldom came back. He had to make do with one or two weekends a year in the Sierras.

Seth's second son, Ernie, was named after a friend. Both were dead. His son for close to thirty years now. Killed in action, the letter from the Army had said. Shot in an engagement against the Germans in France. Buried someplace in France. A town called Strausbourg. Seth had never seen his grave. Seth had looked up Strausbourg in an encyclopedia. Farm country, it said. A pretty place, he hoped . . . a frown twisted heavily through his stomach . . . but then, what the hell difference did it make?

Seth's eyes moved to Dave McCord, sleeping now.

A man trying to go home.

The old man rested back into his roll, frowning, wishing he didn't like McCord; even more than that, he wished he didn't understand what he was trying to do.

SIXTEEN

Tom Quade drew two cups of coffee from the machine in the hospital hallway, then walked back down to the waiting room.

Ann Rule looked up as he approached. He held out a cup to her.

"Thank you," she said, taking it.

"Sorry to keep you here," the sheriff apologized, sitting down beside her. "Take you over to the house in a bit. Just want to know how Milt's gonna . . ."

The rap of shoes on the hospital tile brought his eyes around. A pretty young nurse smiled down at him.

"Telephone for you, Sheriff. Down here." She pointed the way.

" 'Scuse me, Annie," he said, and handed her his cup. "Don't drink 'em both," he smiled, "machine coffee'll poison you."

He followed the nurse down the hall to the desk and took the phone.

"Tom? Corey," barked the voice on the phone.

The sheriff winced. "Yeah, Corey."

"How's Milt?"

"Don't know yet. Cook's in with him now. How 'bout that call to Denver?"

"McCord's father? Nothin' yet, Tom. Can't seem to locate him."

"Keep tryin'," he said. "And call the highway patrol in Lone Rock. Get me Fred Tolliver."

Hanging up, he saw coming toward him a wiry, balding man dressed in an operating gown. Jack Cook looked like he'd been having a hard time. His eyes were tired, but then they always were.

"How is he, Doc?"

Cook frowned. "Call me Bones, or Pill Roller, or Quinine Jimmy. Even Jack. Always hated bein' called Doc. Reminds me of Bugs Bunny for some reason."

Quade smiled. "I know. How is he, Jack?"

The doctor took a cigarette from a pack in his tunic and lit it. "Broke a leg, two fingers on his left hand, three on the right. Cracked his jaw and there's a lot of internal damage." The doctor spoke in wads of smoke.

Quade swallowed. "He goin' to make it?"

The doctor's eyes creased. "I don't know, Tom. I give him better than even chance."

Quade nodded. "All right, Jack." He tried to smile. "Can't ask better than that."

"Sure you can." Cook frowned.

From the desk a nurse called, "Dr. Cook . . ."

"Yeah?"

"They need you in emergency," she said. "Boy fell—"

Cook was already moving, running back down the hall, throwing away the cigarette.

Quade watched him until he went around a corner. Behind the nurse's desk, the telephone rang.

"Sheriff," the nurse said, holding out the phone to him.

"Hello, Corey," he said.

"How'd you know it was me?"

"Inspiration."

"What?"

"Nothing." Quade shook his head. "What'd you get?"

"Well, that McCord fella's out of town on business. Gave me a number in Jackson, Mississippi, but I couldn't raise him."

"Christ," the sheriff grumbled, "his kid's out there in the Leyenda and he's makin' money."

"Got Tolliver on the other line. You want to talk to him?"

"Yeah." Quade nodded and waited.

"Tom?"

"Hello, Fred," the sheriff said, frowning. "Need to ask you a favor."

"Shoot."

"I'm gonna need some men for a couple of days." He swallowed. "And, Fred, make sure they're armed. . . ." A flicker of movement beside him pulled his eyes around as he spoke and, glancing up, he met Ann Rule's gaze.

"I . . ." she stammered, eyes wide with disbelief, "your coffee was getting cold." The cup trembled in her hand. She stared at the sheriff for a moment; then, shoving it past him to the desk, she turned, hurrying away.

"Tom?" Tolliver's voice buzzed on the line. "Tom? You still there?"

"Damn." The sheriff sighed and pulled the receiver back to his ear. "Yeah, Fred. Listen, I'm gonna have to get back to you."

"Sure, but—"

Hanging up, Quade followed Ann to the waiting room. She sat on a couch.

"Annie . . ."

"You're going to kill him," she whispered.

"Ann," Quade sighed wearily, "I'm not gonna do any such thing. I do have to take precautions."

"Like going after him with guns?"

"Damnit," Quade barked, then pressed back his anger. "I don't like this any more than you do."

"Isn't there any other way?"

Quade frowned. "If I knew of one, I'd try it. But I don't."

Her eyes came up. "What about me?"

"What?"

"Let me go with you to Grass River, Mr. Quade. Maybe I could talk him into giving up. He trusts me. Maybe he would listen to me."

Quade's eyes narrowed. "First you help him escape, now you're sayin' you'd try to talk him into coming in?"

The girl's face shadowed. "I just don't want to see him get hurt."

Quade shook his head. "It's a long shot, Annie. You might not even see him. He—"

"But isn't it worth a try? Isn't it worth it to keep somebody else from getting hurt?"

Quade blinked, then stared at her. "Yeah," he finally said, nodding. "It is. All right, Annie," he sighed, "you can come along. Maybe I need my head examined, but you can come along."

SEVENTEEN

Morning did not come. Only a grayness and a blending of white.

Seth woke and, pulling out of his roll, scratched at the coals of the fire, scattered twigs on them, followed by heavier wood, and began brewing coffee.

Looking to McCord, the old man checked the ropes around his wrists, then slipped out of the lean-to and slogged his way to the horses. The snowfall beneath the wall had been light, most of it blowing out and down the saddle. The horses had foraged some grass and, untying them, Seth led them down the wall and tied them again.

He raised his eyes to the sky. The snow fell in steady, large flakes. Not much wind, the old man mused. Turning back down the incline, he saw the tracks.

He knew what they were before he knelt down.

The wolves again.

Three, it looked like.

Standing, he frowned, and strode back to the lean-to and ducked inside.

McCord rustled in his bag and, poking his head out, blinked sleepily at the old man. His eyes went to the fire and he smiled.

"Coffee," he said.

Nodding, Seth scattered a handful of grounds into the boiling water and removed it from the fire.

"Only good thing about instant," Dave yawned, "is you can have it now."

"But it ain't worth drinkin'," scowled the old man.

Dave's eyes rested on the old man's face as he pushed a frying pan into the flames.

"You're in a good mood this mornin'."

Seth's eyes snapped to his prisoner, then he allowed a nod. "Sorry," he said, shaking his head. "Just came across wolf tracks out there."

Dave sat up, looking into the snow. "Trouble?"

"No," the old man answered, putting the beans on the fire. Then, scooping snow, he scattered it over the coffee grounds to settle them. "Just looking for scraps. They usually won't come this close to a camp, though. They don't like the smell of man." He frowned. "They must be hungry." He looked around at Dave. "Just take it easy and don't open that wound again. We don't need the smell of blood around here." He poured a cup of coffee for Dave and handed it to him.

Taking the coffee, Dave shrugged. "They wouldn't come after two of us."

"No," Seth replied, nodding. "But it might stir 'em up enough to put 'em against the horses. Might not bring them down, but they could cripple one."

Dave sipped his coffee gingerly. "What's the weather look like?"

Seth grinned back at him. "Snow."

Dave returned the smile sourly. "Thanks."

"Not bad," the old man answered, and began stirring the beans. "Not that much wind, but the snow's comin' heavy. May not be a norther at all. We can sit a day and see. You need the rest anyway."

"Yeah." Dave nodded. "You don't want to hand in damaged goods."

Seth's eyes jerked up and Dave frowned. "Sorry," he said, shrugging. "That was a cheap shot."

The old man looked back to his cooking. "Maybe not," he said. He stirred the beans for a minute, then slammed the spoon down into them, looking back at his prisoner. "Look," he said, "I don't like takin' you in any more than you like bein' taken in. You wouldn't've made it anyway. By now Quade's back in

Three Medicine and on his way up to Grass River. If you'da outrun me, you'd still have him to contend with."

"I get the chance, I will." Dave nodded.

"Damn." The old man sighed. "You talk about me bein' hard to get along with. You could give lessons. Face it, son, you're goin' back."

Dave leaned back against the tree, shaking his head.

"Men to ride the river with . . ." he whispered.

"What?"

Dave brought up his eyes. "Men to ride the river with, you said yesterday. Brave men. Mountain dwellers. You were right, Seth. They're all gone. Including you, because you're like all the rest. You've sold out, too. . . ."

It was nearly nightfall when Tom Quade maneuvered his car down the old highway, through the dark snowfall, and into the beginnings of the ghost town.

He glanced at Ann on the seat beside him. She sat quietly, her eyes searching through the whiteness.

Tom frowned. She hadn't said three words during the whole trip up here. She had just ridden, staring out the window.

Old buildings began to drift through the snow like huddled, tired animals. He could only barely make out the sign at the side of the road as he went by it.

GRASS RIVER

"Made it," the sheriff commented.

Ann's only answer was a nod.

The road dropped down a long hill into more buildings. Turning down what had been the main street of the town, Tom counted four highway patrol cars lined along the wooden walk in front of the porch of the old courthouse.

Quade parked behind them. Then, taking two bags from the back seat, he gave one to Ann and they rushed inside. Tom led the way down an empty hall to a small room.

Three men sitting around a wood-burning stove looked up as Quade and Ann came into the room.

Fred Tolliver stood, extending his hand. He was a short, sturdy man with a flat-brimmed patrol hat pushed back on an iron-gray crew cut.

"Tom," he said, then nodded and looked to Ann. "This must be the young fella's friend you told me about on the phone."

Tom introduced them and Ann shook his hand halfheartedly.

"Got a room for you, Miss Rule," Tolliver said, glancing back to the stove. "Matt," he called, "show the young lady down to her room."

One of the men at the stove stood up. "Down here," he said.

"Get settled," Tom said to her. "I'll be back in a bit."

"All right." Ann nodded. "I'd like to rest for a while, I guess." Following the patrolman, she went back out into the hall.

Tolliver watched her leave, then looked to Tom.

"You think she'll do any good?"

Quade smiled wearily and shrugged. "Hell, I don't know, Fred. Nothin' else is goin' right, why should this?"

Tolliver smiled. "Gotta hand it to you, Tom. Even picked good weather for it."

"They didn't elect me sheriff for nothin'," Quade replied, nodding and looking around the room. Besides the stove there were two tables surrounded by chairs, and four cots around the walls. Duffle bags were strewn on the floor and cards had been left on the tables. A homelessness permeated them, wriggling a sudden twist of loneliness through Quade's stomach.

"Coffee?" Tolliver offered.

Quade shook his head. "Not right now," he said. "I'd like to look around."

Pulling on a coat, the patrolman led the way back outside.

"Sorry to get you out like this," the sheriff apologized, ambling back toward the highway.

Tolliver smiled. "I'm the boss," he said. "Tell it to my boys."

Tom grinned. "Would, but it's too cold." The smile faded. "Anything yet?"

Fred Tolliver shook his head grimly. "Nothing. You're sure they'd come out here?"

"With any kind of luck, they could have been out today."

"With luck." Tolliver frowned. "This snow may have stopped 'em."

"What's the word on the weather?"

"Not good. We're catchin' a little of a front right now. But there's another one due through here that may freeze our butts off." He looked at the sheriff. "How much longer you want to give 'em?"

"How long can you stay?"

"Three or four days."

Tom nodded. "That'll have to do." His eyes moved over the dead town. "How've you got it set up?"

Tolliver nodded back toward the courthouse. "Headquarters there." Shifting around, he pointed up the highway. "Got the regular men, two of 'em keepin' an eye out along Forty-one. Two others—off-duty men—on horseback along the rim of the plateau. Plateau's down there to the south." He gestured into the shroud of white. "And that ridge and stand of trees is right up there across the highway and up that old road."

Squinting, Quade could barely make out an old shaked-lined snaking of flat snow.

He nodded. "You've got it covered."

"Hope so." Tolliver shivered, then looked at the sheriff. "Tom . . ."

"Yeah?"

"You said to bring these fellas armed. How dangerous is he?"

Quade frowned. "I'm not sure, Fred."

"How far you want to carry it?"

The sheriff sighed heavily. "I want him given every chance and then some. That's why I brought the girl. Then all I have to go by is the book. He's got a gun, and he's an escaped prisoner. One man has been hurt already. I don't want there to be any more."

Ann thanked the patrolman and, closing the door behind her, put down the bag and restlessly surveyed the small room.

A bed and a stove. Clothes rack on the wall. She held out her hand to the stove. It was warm.

She sat down on the bed, then stretched out on top of the covers and stared at the ceiling. She closed her eyes but couldn't relax.

Standing again, she went back out into the hallway. The men in the first room were talking. She started to go in; then, changing her mind, she walked back to the main door and outside.

Staying beneath the protection of the porch, she watched the snow fall. The white motion almost made her feel calm. There was peace in it. Purity. And death, she reminded herself.

The rap of boots on the wood drew up her eyes. Sheriff Quade and Fred Tolliver were coming up the walk and onto the porch.

Seeing her, Quade hesitated. "Annie—?"

"Just getting some air," she said.

Quade glanced at Tolliver. "Be with you in a minute," he said. Nodding, the patrolman pushed through the door and Quade crossed the porch to the girl.

"Little chilly to be gettin' a breath of air, ain't it?"

Ann smiled. "A little," she acknowledged.

Quade pulled his coat tighter, then looked at the girl. "Havin' second thoughts?"

The smile faded. "I suppose." She nodded.

"You're doin' the right thing," the sheriff assured her.

"I know." She frowned. "At least I guess I know. It's so twisted up, Mr. Quade. Being here makes sense one way, but not another."

Quade smiled and touched her shoulder. "That's the way of it, Annie. Never black or white, always in between."

"With Dave caught in the middle."

The sheriff nodded. "Yeah."

Ann shook her head. "Doesn't anybody ever win, Mr. Quade?"

A heaviness weighted through the sheriff's face. "Not in these times." He sighed. "Not much, at any rate."

Seth poured the last of his coffee and glanced at Dave. He was lying quiet. Most likely asleep, the old man thought. He nodded and, raising his cup to his lips, peered out of the lean-to.

Night blackened the snow. The old man tasted the coffee, frowning. Like somebody'd used chips to settle the grounds.

The day had been a long one.

Seth had again made a day's work of cooking, finding wood, eating and caring for the horses. He measured himself, stretching time so that he wouldn't have too much of it idle.

The thing that got on his nerves wasn't time, but Dave. He hadn't said anything since that morning. He had pulled himself to the edge of the lean-to, sitting there most of the day staring into the falling snow.

The old man tossed the remains of his coffee into the snow and, resting back, started to get into his roll.

"Seth," Dave said, turning a little, looking at the old man.

"Yeah, son?"

"What I said earlier—I'm sorry."

"You got a right—"

"No," the younger man said. "The more I think about it, the more I think I'd do the same thing. I'd take you in, too."

The old man nodded stiffly, the words coming hard. "Maybe we both still have some learnin' to do," he said, and settled back in his roll.

Lying back in his sleeping bag, Dave waited. After twenty minutes he heard the old man's breathing coming regular and low. He waited another hour; then, twisting in his bag as if asleep, he pulled himself up, getting more slack in the rope that bound him to the tree.

His fingers curled into the knots, trying to force a grasp, but the ropes around his wrists held his hands too close. He couldn't get his wrists turned enough to get any real pressure on the knots on the rope to the tree. That was the one he had to get first. The other he could do later.

Jesus, but that old man could tie knots.

His heart hammered as he tried again, his breath catching as he concentrated all his strength to his hands. The bones of his wrists pressed against the hemp, mashing tendons until he thought he was going to cry out. Trembling, he let his breath ease out down into the bag. He looked at the knots again in the flickering light from the fire. He lay back for a time, staring up at the pine bough ceiling; then, pulling up a little more, he went to work again.

EIGHTEEN

Just before dawn, his hands slipped free of the rope holding him to the tree.

Shivering with exhaustion, Dave lay back down into his bag, drenched with sweat, and looked at the ropes still binding his hands.

It would have to wait.

Turning quietly, Dave's eyes moved over the rise of his own body to Seth's sleeping hulk.

Wriggling his hands down, Dave unzipped the bag slowly, carefully, then sat up.

Seth didn't move.

Dave squinted, picking out of the darkness the shapes of the rifles. He felt his breath thicken in his chest, numbing him.

He had to get across Seth to get to a rifle. Swallowing, and pressing back his fear, he leaned toward the old man.

Seth rustled in his blankets, thrusting up a shoulder.

Dave hesitated, hanging in mid-air, hovering above the old man. Easing back, he sat down for a moment. He looked from the rifles, outside, and back to the rifles again.

Frowning and shaking his head, he picked up his hat and, tugging his legs free of the sleeping bag, he pushed himself up and slipped outside.

The snow had thinned back into a wandering vagueness, blurring the light to the east. The cold stopped Dave for a moment. He had gotten used to the warmth of the sleeping bag and the lean-to.

Pulling up the collar of his coat, he scanned the trees until he picked out the horses, then started for them, his hip stiff, beginning to throb as he moved. Limping, and slightly off balance because of his hands, Dave waded through the knee-deep snow.

The horses jerked as he came toward them, Seth's dun snorting and moving away from him. The sorrel pumped his back legs, tautening the rope holding him.

Dave halted. "Easy," he whispered to the horses. "Easy, down."

Moving gently, he stepped out again.

The sorrel crow-hopped, whinnying.

"Easy," Dave whispered urgently. "Jesus, be quiet."

In the lean-to, Seth jerked awake, knowing he'd heard something but not knowing what.

Tense, he lay quiet, straining his ears. Then he heard the horses again.

"Wolves," he muttered, bolting up, his hands grasping his Henry, tearing his legs from the roll. Halfway up, he saw that Dave's bag was empty.

"Goddamnit," he barked, rushing forward, slamming through the reflector, shattering it. He charged around the lean-to, bringing up the Henry.

Through the trees, he caught a flicker of red.

"Dave!" he shouted, running.

Seth's voice jerked Dave like electricity. Tearing at the sorrel's halter rope, he ripped it free. The sorrel reared slightly. Rushing the animal, and holding the rope, Dave buried his hands in his mane. The sorrel was still moving, wheeling around, beginning to run.

Still holding on to the mane, Dave clung to the horse as he hauled him down the hill, ramming through brush and low limbs. A pine bough pounded into his chest, hammering him back, but he held on.

Desperately he tried to pull himself up. But he slipped and his feet touched the ground. He ran a few steps with the horse, then, springing off the ground, he managed to hang his arm over the sorrel's back and drag himself up, falling sideways across the running animal. The horse's shoulders pounded him in the stomach and, twisting, he tried to pull himself around.

The sorrel crashed through the trees and into the open, exploding into a full gallop. Dave clawed at the mane, trying to pull himself up at the same time, but the horse gained speed.

Getting his right leg up, Dave began pulling himself around.

The sorrel burst over the bank of a creekbed, and suddenly the horse seemed to be falling under him. Dave grasped the neck, and the sorrel sidestepped, twisting under him, throwing Dave out to one side.

He was falling, his fingers raking across the animal's neck. Still holding the rope, Dave tipped off the horse, plunging into the snow. Groping wildly, he closed his fist on the rope. Running, the horse dragged Dave through the snow. Dave screamed, trying to haul the animal back around when something hard smashed into his shoulder, stunning him, forcing his hands open, letting the rope slice through them and away.

He slumped down, lying still in the snow for a moment, the sound of the horse's running still in him, mingling with the pain from his hip. Reaching down, he could feel his leg wet with blood again.

"Seth," he whispered. Dragging himself up, he looked back up the hill.

No sign of the old man yet. But there would be.

Pushing himself up, he began limping down the creekbed.

Seth hurdled down through the trees, following the tracks. He'd lost sight of McCord almost immediately. Rushing out of the trees, he pushed across the open ground to the creekbed and, hesitating, combed the horizon for any sign of the running man.

Nothing. He frowned. He would have to go back up and get Nate. Turning, he saw something in the snow. Blood. The old man's eyes moved back over the ground.

Must be getting old, he scowled.

McCord had been thrown, and dragged a short distance. A faint line of blood colored his course.

Seth shook his head and looked up. "Jesus, son," he murmured, his voice lost in the wind. "Don't you know when you've had it?"

Dave ran.

Chewing at the knots on the rope around his wrists, he slogged through the snow, his hip aching, the blood freezing to the pant leg. At least it had stopped most of the bleeding, and the rest had helped it some.

He pushed up a long hill and came out above a long, horseshoe-shaped valley. Below him, the sides jutted down steeply. Sitting, still chewing at the ropes, he looked for easy ground, following the hill to where it fell into the valley.

Long way, he thought. Long . . .

Looking back behind him, he remembered something Seth had told him. A man on foot could go places a man on a horse couldn't.

Dave looked back down the steep valley wall and smiled.

"Thanks, Seth," he said, nodding. Edging over the side, he began slipping his way down the incline. He moved quickly at first, finding footholds, and running, catching himself with his hands.

Then he was going too fast, momentum pushing at his back, thrusting him down the side until he lost his footing, stumbling, diving down the slope, sliding to a rest at the bottom.

Rolling over, he pulled himself up and began to walk again, forcing the knots back to his mouth. He had to get them off. He might have been all right on that incline if he'd had his hands.

Stumbling, he fell again and, trying to rise, slumped down in the snow.

He had to rest some time. A little. And he had to get off those damn ropes.

Sitting up, his breath cawed through him and the sound

frightened him a little. It was more like an animal's sound than a man's.

He looked to the ropes and, twisting them, went to work on the knots.

The hemp cut into his lips and gums and after a while he could taste the blood. He worked calmly, methodically, tugging the ropes, easing them, finally breaking one of the knots. Hurrying then, he bit the ropes and twisted his wrists until the ropes gave and then fell off.

He was free.

Smiling and shivering, he stood up, looking back over his shoulder to see if Seth—

Something moved in the trees.

His breath caught and he turned, straining to pick out the movement again. It wasn't Seth, he knew that.

There was no wind. Only a stillness lacing the trees as tangible as the cold pressing through him.

And he saw the first one.

The old man broke camp, leaving most of Dave's gear, saving only his sleeping bag and rifle.

Mounting Nate, Seth peered up at the sky. The snow had nearly stopped falling and it wasn't quite as cold as it had been. Maybe it would hold. The old man sighed, thinking of Dave on foot. Then, turning Nate down the hill, he rode back to the creekbed and began to follow the fugitive's tracks.

He was coming out of the creekbed when he saw the first tracks. A few at first, then a collection of them speckling the ground. Following the blood.

A harsh shudder cracked through the old man's body.

"My God . . ." he whispered.

NINETEEN

Dave McCord had never seen wolves this close before.

Just dead, hanging from fence posts. And one a long time ago running away.

This one wasn't running away and he wasn't dead. He came to the edge of the pines and sat down, watching Dave. Waiting.

A chill thickening to nausea washed through the man. Now he knew where the myth about them came from.

A mixture of horror and beauty.

His coat was rough, thick, gray-black. He resembled a dog in shape only. He was nothing like a dog in the way he waited and watched. Primed, uncowering, eyes alive, aware of each movement the man made.

Dave was nearly hypnotized by him for a moment, then a flicker of movement in the corner of his eye jerked his head around.

Another wolf emerged from the trees. White, followed by another gray-black, smaller than the first. Sitting down, they watched him.

Waiting, too.

Trembling, Dave swallowed, struggling to keep the coiling panic in his stomach from spreading.

He had to walk.

As long as he was on his feet he was all right.

Dave made himself turn, putting his back to them, and began to walk, wanting to run. But he couldn't do that. He had to stay on his feet long enough to get to Grass River.

Walking, he glanced back up the hill. The wolves stayed

there until he started up the next slope, then the larger gray-black followed slowly.

Dave brought his eyes back around.

"Walk," he said aloud. "Just keep walking."

Seth strapped Nate hard, running him up a long hill, topping the crest above a small valley. The wall of it fell away sharply beneath him, and he could see where Dave had started down, and then probably fallen. The wolf tracks followed.

"Damn," the old man growled. He would never get a horse down that slope. Wheeling Nate out, he ran for the nearest end of the valley.

"Too long," he whispered to himself, the frustration hammering at him.

Thirty minutes later he turned down the southern end of the valley and began threading his way back toward Dave's tracks.

Dave walked up the northern end of the valley, weaving, struggling to keep himself upright.

The valley lifted toward a gathering of hills, and beyond them a set of peaks. He came up over a small knoll and around a downed trunk, a dead limb thrusting up like a dead, pointing arm.

The hill lifted more and, reaching out, Dave found himself crawling, scraping up the slope on all fours.

"No," he murmured, standing and nearly toppling backward.

He looked down the hill.

The wolves came around the knoll and sat down.

Staring at them, Dave tried to rest while standing. His stillness weighted through him, whispering him toward the ground.

He felt himself weaving and, widening his legs, looked down at the wolves again.

Strangely, there was nothing malevolent about them. Nothing evil. No game. Just the fact that he was food to them and nothing more.

That frightened him more than anything else.

Trembling, he concentrated on standing. For a moment he thought that he might be able to sit, then shook his head; that might be the same death trap as sleeping in the snow.

Turning, he stumbled and, pushing himself, pulled his legs forward, dragging his feet through the snow.

A line of trees brushed through the mist at the rop of the rise, a hundred yards away now.

A deadly heaviness bled through his legs, arms, and shoulders, blending with the pain from his hip and the aching cold of raw air in his lungs.

Stumbling again, he fell and forced himself up.

"Tired," he whispered, then tried to think of the line of trees, the peaks beyond, and the plateau on the other side. They were there. The high country was there. He could hide in Grass River, rest, then go on. Not far away. Not a day's walk now.

Staggering, he pitched forward in the snow. Lying still for a moment, then getting his hands under him, he shoved himself over, facing downslope.

The wolves sat down below him, just above the small knoll.

Dave's eyes searched frantically over the slope, stopping on the branch jutting up from the downed trunk.

Fumbling his feet under him, Dave crawl-walked back down to the trunk. Down the slope the wolves backed away a few feet and sat down again. Resting on the log, Dave leaned against the limb and closed his eyes for a moment.

"Damn," he said, sighing. Opening his eyes, he looked at the branch. It was about five feet long, eight inches thick at the trunk, tapering up to the size of Dave's fist. Make a good club, the man thought, frowning, except that the wood was dead.

"All I've got," he whispered. Reaching up, using the branch, Dave pulled himself to a standing position; then, grasping the limb with both hands and straightening his arms, he lunged against it. The limb held. Trembling, his breath raking through him, he leaned on the branch. Then, looking up at it and holding his breath, he closed his hands around the limb again, walking against it. The sound of the wood cracking barked like a shot, then it gave. Still holding the branch, Dave nearly fell. He tripped against the trunk and, dropping the branch, caught himself.

Dragging his legs around, he slumped down on the trunk and picked up the heavy branch, laying it across his legs.

He raised his eyes. The wolves were still there.

He looked back up toward the trees and shook his head. No need to waste the strength. Besides, he thought, pushing his eyes back down the slope, from here he would be able to see them coming. Open ground all around him.

Easing down into the snow, he put his back against the log. A darkness of fatigue and pain rushed up at him, engulfing him, pulling him into itself. Near-dreams, halves twisted, whorling, weaving him into a pocket of time, and for a moment he thought he was with Heck again. Riding. Moving . . .

And something touched him.

He smelled the wolf before he saw him. Sharp. Raw.

His body slammed taut, his eyes snapped open.

A wolf, the large gray-black, was at his feet.

Jerking the club, Dave caught him in the shoulder, surprising him, and sprawling the wolf backward. Yelping, the wolf twisted in the snow and Dave lunged, raking the club with a half-blow into the wolf's shoulder again, tumbling him over onto his back.

His teeth slashing, the gray-black snapped at the wood. Crawling toward him, Dave hit him in the ribs. The wolf scrambled and clawed to his feet, diving at the man.

Arching the club up, Dave caught him in mid-air, pounding the wood into the gray-black's chest, splintering the club in two, crushing the wolf to the ground.

The stunned animal writhed in the snow. Raising the three-foot stub he had left, Dave moved toward him.

White flashed in the corner of his eye and, reeling, the man swept the stub around at a second wolf charging his legs. Dave slammed him across the mouth but the white wolf kept coming, snapping, tearing at the wood, ripping through the man's gloves.

Screaming, Dave tried to step back, and the wolf charged.

Hauling the club around, Dave cracked the white wolf in the head, shattering what was left of his club, knocking the animal to the ground.

The man flung away the scrap of wood, and, falling on the wolf, hit him in the snout with his fist, beating him back into the snow, ignoring the weakening teeth bloodying his hands. Grasping its foot, he lifted the dazed animal, swinging him around high in the air, then hurled him down into the log. The sound of shattering wood and bones cracked down the slope as Dave stepped into the wolf and kicked through its jaws, smashing its head.

Still holding the wolf's leg, the man pivoted, flinging around the dead hulk and throwing it down the hill at the third running wolf.

Off to the man's left, the large gray-black was scrambling to his feet, following his companion over the rise. Then they were gone.

Trembling, the man looked down at his bleeding hands and the webs of blood latticed around him.

"Jesus," he whispered, sinking to his knees. "What—"

A sound jerked up his eyes. Below the rise, out of sight. He pushed himself to his feet and waited.

"Come on," he growled, tensing. "Come on."

A hat came slowly above the rise. Then Seth emerged, coming up the knoll.

"Nothin'," Dave whispered, sitting down. "All for nothin'."

TWENTY

Seth helped Dave up the slope to the trees. Then, sitting him down, he looked at Dave's hands.

"You're lucky, son," he said, taking out his hunting knife.

Dave frowned. "You gonna tie 'em again?"

The old man's eyes came up darkly. "Have to." He nodded. "You know that."

Slipping the knife into Dave's gloves, he carefully cut away what was left of them. There were slashes on them, but only the small finger on the left hand had been badly cut.

"Gloves saved 'em," the old man observed. "Got another pair and some medicine in my bags," he said as he stood and turned to his horse.

Dave's eyes followed him up, then went to Nate and the two rifle butts showing in the scabbard.

Seth was still turning as Dave bolted up, jacking his elbow into the old rancher's back, shoving him forward, throwing him down the slope, plowing through the snow.

Running, Dave got to the horse, jerked out the Henry, levered it, and brought it around on the old man.

"What the—" he sputtered, and his eyes stopped on the rifle. "You bastard," he whispered. "I was tryin' to help you."

"I know," Dave said, nodding, "and I'm sorry, Seth."

The old man's anger eased and he stood up slowly, shaking his head. "It's come down to it, ain't it, son?"

Dave centered the rifle on Seth's chest. "Looks that way, doesn't it?"

The old man pointed at the rifle. "I'm bettin' you won't shoot me."

"You'd lose." Dave's mouth hardened. "I won't kill you, but I'll cripple you, Seth. Don't make me do it."

The old man looked at the rifle, then raised his eyes to Dave. "All right, son." He nodded, relaxing. "What's it gonna be?"

"I'm gonna have to borrow your horse."

"Borrow?"

"Yes, borrow, goddamnit," Dave snapped. "He'll be waitin' for you in Grass Valley, along with your rifle."

Edging down toward the horse, Dave untied the food bag and Seth's bedroll, dropping them to the ground. Turning to Nate, he mounted the horse.

"You might make it in tomorrow," he said to the old man.

"I will," Seth said, nodding.

Dave stared down at the old man and, looking at his hands, saw that they were trembling. He pushed his eyes back to Seth.

"You won't even ask, will you?"

"Beg you, son?" Seth shook his head. "No. It wouldn't do no good no how. It's the only way you'll make it. You have to leave me."

Dave's eyes held on the old man for another moment, then he frowned. "Sorry," he said quietly. Reeling the dun out, he pushed him up the slope through the trees and over the crest.

The old man watched Dave sink over the crest.

"Damn," he whispered tightly. "Goddamn."

Glancing through the trees, he shook his head, then went to scrounging up firewood. He scraped a place in the snow, started the fire, then opened a can of stew and put it on to warm.

His eyes wandered to the sky.

If it held he would make it easily tomorrow. He looked at the crest again and frowned.

McCord had beaten him. And he had lost it all.

Dave rode Nate hard down the other side of the crest, pushing him toward the peaks. His hands and his hip ached, but even with that he felt like laughing.

Then, looking down at the Henry across the saddle, he remembered the old man. Frowning, he jammed the rifle down into the scabbard with the 30.06.

He'd done what he'd had to do.

The horse moved under him, carrying him away from the old man and toward the high country.

"He'll be all right," the fugitive whispered to himself, repeating the words, closing his eyes tightly as if saying them again would make them true.

Opening his eyes, he saw the rifle under his leg.

"Not my worry, goddamnit," he said aloud. "The old bastard isn't my worry."

Pushing Nate out, Dave ran him up the deep hills, pulling for the peaks, coming around the edge of them, skirting a canyon to one side, coming up the shoulder of the mountains, through a stand of boulders, and into the open again.

Reining in, Dave looked down the long slopes to the open country and up again, trying to pick out the plateau Seth had been talking about.

Odd, he thought, swinging his eyes over the horizon.

There was nothing, only blue-white darkness to the north and west.

His stomach twisted with realization.

"Another front," he whispered. Shifting in the saddle, he traced it around to the north until it disappeared behind the mountains.

Resting back down in the saddle, his leg brushed the Henry and, staring at it, he shook his head. He raised his eyes to the front again.

The old man would have a helluva walk through that.

Leaning forward on the saddle horn, Dave touched the rifle.

"Not my concern," he whispered. "Not . . ." Frowning, he shook his head. It was no use. "You old bastard," he growled, twisting Nate angrily back around. "Damn!" Spurring the horse, Dave ran back along the shoulder. "Stupid," he swore. "The old man was right, I am a fool. . . ."

The old man had inched his way down the slope and started up the hills toward the peaks when he saw the darkness against the snow a mile away. Moving toward him.

Squinting, he hesitated. "Dave?" he said aloud.

He smiled suddenly and felt like running. Instead, he shouldered his roll and the food sack and walked.

The darkness grew slowly, becoming a rider and a horse. The horse was a dun.

Dropping his gear to the ground, the old man sat down on a rock and waited.

Dave took his time, walking Nate in and up to the old man.

"Seth." He nodded.

The old man couldn't keep the smile off his lips. He let it come grudgingly.

"I'll be damned," he said, sighing.

"So will I." Dave nodded. "I'm not feelin' very bright today." He looked down at the old man. "You gonna sit there all day?"

"No, I guess not." Seth stretched up, standing, then hesitated, his eyes narrowed. "Why the hell did you come back, son?"

"Front." Dave pointed back over his shoulder. "Saw it on the other side of the peaks."

"Bad?"

"It's not good."

"Damn." The old man sighed and started toward Dave.

"One thing," the young man said, stopping him, "I want your word you won't try and put those ropes back on me until we get to Grass River."

"Or?"

"Or I'll turn and ride out of here."

The old man smiled. "You mean you'll take my word?"

Dave grinned. "Yeah, Seth," he nodded, "I'll take your word. Now can I have it so we can get out of here?"

"Yeah," Seth gave up a nod slowly, "you've got my word. To Grass River."

TWENTY-ONE

Riding double, the two men pushed up the slopes and around the shoulder of the peaks along the canyon.

In front Seth guided Nate through the boulders, then to the face overlooking the open country. His mouth tugged down into a heavy frown as he saw what Dave had described to him.

The front was coming like a great wave, rushing down from the north, blending everything into itself.

"Jesus," the old man whispered. "A five-day blow at least."

"Want to try for the lean-to?"

"No." Seth shook his head. "We're better off heading for Grass River. Our food'd never last through that."

Turning back the dun along the face and around the shoulder, he stopped in the run of boulders.

"Here," he said to Dave, and the young man slipped off.

They made camp quickly, finding a spot deep in the giant rocks.

"Eat all we can tonight and in the mornin'," Seth said, starting the food and coffee. "We're not goin' to be able to have a fire out there, anyway. We'll have to make it on jerky"—he held up a thermos—"and coffee."

He went back to his cooking and was dishing it out when he heard the wind. "Hear it?" he asked, his head coming up like a deer's.

Dave nodded stiffly. "Yeah," he said. "I hear it."

"Looks like the Leyenda has a little more in store for us."

Dave nodded wordlessly. The old man eyed him for a moment, then went on talking. "Them wolves musta given you a time."

Beyond the rocks, the pitch of the wind was rising.

The old man handed Dave his plate. "Son . . ." he said.

The young man looked around. "What—oh, thanks," he said, taking the plate.

"You done a good job against them wolves," the old man said.

Dave shrugged, his eyes concentrating on what was on the other side of the rocks.

"How is it?" Seth asked, nodding at the food.

"All right."

"Could be better." Seth frowned, pushing another forkful into his mouth.

Dave chewed his food for a minute, then asked, "How far?"

"Grass River? Across the plateau. A day unless we miss the way up, then it'll be a little rough. We'd have to go west around it. That'd take another day."

"There a trail?"

"Not really a trail, no." The old man shook his head. "Just where the river comes down the cliffs. We can get part way up followin' it, then cuttin' over to one side for about the last two hundred feet."

"Cut over?"

"There's a falls at the top."

Dave nodded and finished eating, then put down his plate and poured coffee for them both. The sound of the wind grew, wrapping around them.

"How's your hip?" Seth asked.

"Fine."

"Your hands?"

"Fine," Dave snapped. Then, frowning, he added, "They're both sore."

"Can you do some walkin'?"

"Yeah." The young man nodded.

Darkness came. Dave was in his bag and Seth was in his sleeping roll before nightfall. The fire clawed at the flakes.

Seth watched the huge flakes tumbling over the rocks and listened to the scream of the wind increasing, feeling the fear stretching in him. Darkness bled over them, mingling through the flakes, and the razor sound of the wind trembled in him.

"Seth," the young man said.

Seth looked up. "Yeah?"

Dave stared at him for a moment, then shook his head. "Nothing," he whispered, slumping back in his bag. "Nothing."

The old man sat up, looking at his companion. His mouth attempted a slow smile. "That's two of us," he said. Lying back down in his blankets, he tried to sleep.

TWENTY-TWO

Seth slept fitfully. The wind increased steadily all night, and the old man couldn't seem to push it away far enough to sleep. He sat up the next morning, his muscles knotted and stiff. As soon as he rose from his blankets, Dave did the same. Weary eyes and wooden movements showed that he hadn't slept either.

The two men went about their chores wordlessly.

Seth built the fire back up to a small blaze and prepared the coffee. Dave opened the last four cans of stew and poured them into a skillet, then put it on the fire. While the food cooked, both men rolled their sleeping gear and tied it on Nate.

Returning to the fire, Dave took the skillet and coffeepot from the flames and dished one portion into a plate. He took the skillet for himself. Seth poured coffee and sipped it, then picked up his plate and began shoveling the food into his mouth.

After the first mouthful, he sighed and ate more slowly.

Across the fire, Dave looked at the food sourly and started to put it down.

"Eat," the old man said.

"Not hungry." Dave grimaced.

"You will be. Eat it."

Frowning, and knowing that the old man was right, Dave picked up the skillet and started again.

"Remind me never to eat stew again." The old man chewed. "Needs somethin'."

"Yeah." Seth nodded, forcing himself to eat. "You ever eat prime rib and oysters?"

Dave looked up. "Oysters. Mountain oysters?"

"Hell no." The old man grinned. "Sea oysters."

"You're kidding . . ."

"No, got a lot of cayenne pepper and lemon juice in it."

Dave grinned, then laughed. "Seth, you lyin' old—"

"I'm not," the old man swore. "Does sound terrible, don't it? But it's really got a kick to it." He finished his food and put down his plate.

"Where the hell'd you come up with that?"

The old man sipped his coffee. "Ain't always been in these hills, you know."

Dave finished his portion and the two men drank their coffee. The laughter had slipped away from them.

The old man poured the rest from the pot into the thermoses, then put them in his saddlebags. He washed the plate and skillet, put them into the food bag, then, saving the small grain sack, he cached it down between two rocks.

"Dead weight," he explained to Dave, and turned to the horse. Opening the sack, he fed Nate the last handsful of oats.

"That's it for a spell." He sighed. "May have to scratch a little." He looked to Dave. "We'll walk awhile. Best not to tire him all of a sudden. You take one side, I'll do the other."

Dave moved around the horse and grabbed the saddle horn.

The old man stared at him for a minute. "There are times" —he winked—"I wish I was someplace else."

Dave smiled and nodded. "That's two of us."

The old man's eyes softened, and he pulled them away quickly. "Nate," he said to the horse.

And walking on both sides of the dun, the two men slogged back around the shoulder, along the canyon, back to the face of the mountain.

The wind hit Dave like a hammer.

Halting, the young man stood as if he were on the edge of a chasm.

He could see nothing before him but white. He knew the distance was there, but he couldn't see it. The colorless void twisted above and below him, and for a moment he thought he was being drawn into it.

"The riverbed," the old man shouted, "is directly below us. Let's go find it."

Dave stared into the void. Lifting his feet, he forced himself to move, beginning his descent.

Across the saddle from Dave, Seth shivered hard, the warmth from the food and coffee gone, cut away by the wind. His hand gripped the saddle horn until it ached, bleeding back up through his arm, brittled by age.

The wind raked across him and he was nearly blind going down the slope. Seth envied Nate's unmindfulness of the whole thing, his acceptance of the way things were, and the way he just kept moving. He wondered if the animal could remember warmth or if he cared. Oats and feed seemed to be the only thing in his memory span. And pain.

The ground fell away under him now, and they were moving faster. Stepping down over a small embankment, Nate started to run and, stumbling, the old man tugged back on the reins.

He looked at Dave. "All right?" he shouted. A stiff nod was his only answer.

Holding on to the saddle, they started again. Walking, Dave glanced at Seth. He seemed to be a long way away.

Shaking his head, Dave looked forward again. They came to the bottom of the slope and stopped.

The old man's eyes moved through the snow, then he pointed. "This way."

The snow clawed at Dave's feet, dragging pain from his hip, and the young man found himself leaning against Nate, holding himself up with the saddle. His leg jerked stiffly through the snow and his hand closed on the pommel.

The wind battered him and his fingers felt like something not a part of him, appendages of glass. Turning his face from the wind, he hugged against the horse, and his foot slipped on a rock. Suddenly his leg was twisting, giving under him. Reeling, he rammed into Nate, then slumped into the snow.

The horse crow-hopped away from him, pounding into Seth. The old man jumped forward, keeping his hands on the reins.

Pulling the horse to him, he calmed him and went back to Dave.

"The hip?" he asked, yelling at the top of his lungs.

Dave pushed himself up, nodding.

"I can make it," he said.

The old man pointed to the horse. "Ride awhile."

Dave shook his head. "No," he protested, "I—"

"Listen," the old man barked. "Get on the goddamn horse. You keep walking, you'll be in worse shape. Kill yourself and maybe me. And I don't like this place well enough to die here. Now get on him."

Surrendering with a nod, Dave slogged to Nate and hauled himself into the saddle.

Dave took the reins and Seth came around Nate, getting the horse between him and the wind. Grasping the horn, he nodded and Dave nudged the animal.

In the saddle, for a moment Dave thought that the wind was going to tear him from it. He kept expecting it to ease a little, but it never did. He never knew anything could be so constant.

They moved up, and then suddenly down into a swath in the earth. The riverbed.

Seth stayed to one side of the middle. He didn't know whether there was any water in the bed, and he didn't want to find out.

The wind pounded Dave.

To keep from thinking about it, Dave concentrated on the movement of the horse beneath him, and the man walking. The man walking was seventy years old, and he was twenty, and it was he who was riding. The man walking strode out, strong, seemingly unmindful of the wind.

Dave suddenly wondered how long they had been out there, jerking with the realization that he had no idea. Time was gone. There was only the old man walking, the horse, the wind, and him, all warped together somehow. Time didn't exist, only their movement, only the reach and strain of muscles, and pain in his hip. The old man suddenly seemed both a long way away and very close. As if Dave could feel his breathing and his dying at the same time. Looking up into the whorling snow, Dave trembled, and dropped his eyes to the old man walking. Moving. Pushing through the wind, bound for the other side.

Going home.

And Dave wondered if he would ever go home.

Slowly, he felt the ground rising under him, and his heart thickened in his chest.

"Seth," he called.

"Yeah?"

"We're goin' up."

"Yeah."

The slope lifted sharply under them, the rocks in the bed growing larger. Dave could feel the horse pulling hard. The ground around them began to fall away steeply, plunging into a swirl of snow and wind.

Nate was at an angle under him now, and Seth moved out in front, taking the bridle and leading the horse. As they went up the bed narrowed, forcing them in toward the middle. Testing the snow, Seth went out on it carefully, getting off it when he could, and staying to the rocks for footing.

They went up. Climbing slowly. Around boulders. Through dead brush. Moving higher. Dave stayed in the saddle, and the old man walked, on his knees sometimes, tugging the horse onward.

Lifting his eyes, Dave could see nothing, but he knew they were making headway. Getting there.

They struggled over a deep chest of rock. Nate reached for a foothold, but his back feet stamped through the snow, and it gave, sinking into a pool of water. Holding on to the horn, Dave stayed in the saddle, and the old man ahead of the horse pulled him on and over the rock.

Dave guessed they had come a little over a half mile since starting up the riverbed, when Seth had started off to one side.

"Falls up ahead," the old man shouted back. "Slope over here."

Pushing over a small rise, they worked their way along a wide slope and into a gathering of pine and aspen.

"Not far," the old man yelled as they came out of the trees. "Just . . ."

His voice was lost in the wind as he halted, staring ahead.

Following his gaze, Dave saw it, too.

A wall of snow thirty feet high.

TWENTY-THREE

Dave dismounted and, walking out, stood with Seth.

"Slide," the old man whispered.

"Any way around it?"

"Not that I know of."

Dave rubbed his chin. "Over it?"

The old man shook his head. "Too deep. 'Sides that, any movement out there's liable to get it started again." He turned, looking back through the trees. "Our only chance is that way."

"Where?"

The old man frowned. "Up the falls," he said. Leading Nate, he walked back through the timber, then along the riverbed until he came to two large rocks forming a V. Climbing up on the larger one, he examined the space between them, then came back to the horse and began to loosen the cinch.

Dave felt a tightness in his chest. "You leavin' him?"

"Have to." The old man nodded. "No way to get him up there."

He hauled off the saddle and carried it to the rocks. Resting it for a moment, he untied the saddlebags and the rope and tossed them to one side. Then he took out the Henry and put it down carefully.

"You gonna be able to carry that?" Dave pointed to the rifle.

"I am, or I'm not gonna make it at all."

"It worth it?"

"Money-wise, no. Only about five hundred. It's all I got left. Goddamn country's taken ever'thin' else. I'm not quittin' this, too."

Crawling back up the rocks, the old man lifted the saddle and stowed it between them, spreading out his bedroll over it.

"Made that myself," he whispered. Turning back down the rocks and picking up the Henry, he looked at Nate.

"I'll take the bags," Dave said, reaching down and hoisting them up to his shoulder. He looked to the old man. "You ready?"

"In a minute." The old man frowned, his eyes still on Nate. Levering the rifle, he stepped toward the horse.

"Seth?" Dave said, unbelieving.

Approaching the horse, Seth began to raise the rifle.

"Seth," Dave screamed, charging down the hill, grasping the old man's coat, jerking him around. Wheeling, the old man twisted up his fist, smashing it across Dave's face, knocking the young man backward, sprawling in the snow.

"You think I want to kill him?" Seth's voice trembled, then quieted. "He hasn't got a prayer out here."

"He's got a right to try."

The old man's eyes glistened wetly. "He won't make it," he whispered. "Better this way."

Dave stood up.

"We might not, either. But as long as we're alive we've got a chance."

The old man's eyes drifted to the horse and, sighing, he shook his head. "Hell, I don't know if I could have shot him anyway." Looking at the horse, he smiled. "You're a tough old bastard," he said. "Write if you find work," he whispered.

His eyes pulled to Dave, the softness gone.

"Let's get out of here," he said.

They started up again.

Scrambling up the shale and pebbles, through house-sized boulders.

The old man climbed mercilessly, never looking back, but Dave couldn't keep from it. The horse seemed to draw his eyes around.

The dun stood watching them, and Dave wondered if it

wouldn't have been better to shoot him. Then the wind smashed across them, carrying a flurry of snow, and the dun was gone.

Dave stopped.

Ahead of him the old man was still climbing.

Dave pulled his eyes around. Up the hill. The old man pushed himself up between a rock and a sapling birch.

"Damn." The younger man swallowed and, hurrying, he caught up with Seth.

Seth angled off the bed and up the bank through a tangle of brush, came out again, then stopped.

"The falls," he said, pointing into the snow.

Lifting his eyes, Dave could barely see the wall of rock. Metal-gray on white rising above them, then blending away.

Breathing heavily, Seth slipped the saddlebags from Dave's shoulder and took the thermoses of coffee from them. He knelt down in the snow and poured two cups. The brief smell of coffee jerked through Dave and Seth gave him one. The warmth from the plastic was like impotent needles. His hands trembled as he raised the cup to his lips. The liquid burned his mouth and, wincing, he spilled some down his front and into the snow. Bringing the cup back, he tried again, forcing it through his numb lips.

"G-good," the young man stuttered.

Seth nodded his agreement and, reaching into the saddlebags again, he produced two strips of jerky. He handed one to Dave and bit into the other.

They ate in silence. Finishing the coffee, Seth put the thermoses back in the saddlebags and laid them aside. Laying out a piece of rope, he cut off a length and tied it to the Henry's stock and barrel, then strung it around his shoulders and stood up.

"Seth . . ."

"Yeah, son?"

"I'm—sorry I got you into this."

A faint smile tugged at the old man's lips.

"I'm of age," he said, nodding. "'Sides, my greed had a little to do with it." Turning, he looked to the falls. "I'll lead," he said.

The two men climbed back down into the riverbed and up the rocks. The boulders had become massive. The old man moved surefootedly over the backs of the rocks and their sleeping skin of white. Saplings and old trunks grew between the boulders and the men used them as footholds to push themselves up.

Soon Dave realized that they were no longer moving horizontally, but up. Above them, the rocks pushed together, blending in a giant weaving of stone.

Looking down, he could no longer see the bottom, only whorls of snow and the rock reaching into it. He dragged his eyes back up. The old man was crawling, scraping over the face of a boulder. He followed him, finding a foothold on the stone and pushing himself up.

Seth topped the boulder and stopped, the air burning his nose and lungs. He glanced back as Dave came up beside him.

Swallowing air, he stood on top of the boulder and walked across it to another thrusting upward. The face was sheer and covered the area of the boulder they stood on.

Seth walked back and forth a couple of times, squinting upward into the wash of snow. His eyes caught on a twist in the whiteness and, stopping, he uncoiled the rope, flicking a noose in the end of it.

"Small pine," the old man guessed. Swinging the loop over his head, he flung it upward. The rope jutted out, then rattled back down on them. The old man tried again, and it hung. Drawing the rope taut, he put all his weight down on it, pulling hard. The rope held.

Wordlessly the old man began climbing, holding the rope and walking up the face of the rock. He made it to the tree and crouched beside it. The loop had caught in the small, gnarled branches. Bringing up some slack, the old man pushed the loop down onto the trunk.

Standing, he yelled back down the slope, "Start comin'."

Below Seth, Dave barely heard him. Going to the rope, he

started up. Leaning back. Taking the weight on his hands. The rope mashed into them and, as he started up, he could feel the wolf cuts being crushed open.

"Jesus," he whispered, stopping and looking up. He couldn't see the old man.

Reaching out, he closed his hand on the rope again. Taking the weight again. The pain jolted through his arms and it was all he could think about. He forgot about his feet for a moment and, slipping, slammed to his knees, hammering the rope into his hands. Blood wet his gloves.

"Dave?" he heard the old man call.

"My hands," he shouted. Shoving his feet back under him, he managed to stand.

The rope began tugging and Dave walked, the rope pulling him.

Above him the old man materialized in the blur of snow. Hauling in the rope, Seth's hands worked mechanically and Dave, holding on, rushed up the face of the boulder and nearly hit the old man as he came up to him, then slumped in the snow.

"You all right?" the old man asked.

Dave nodded. "Hands," he choked.

Taking them, the old man looked at them. "Bleedin' some," he said.

Dave shook his head. "Don't know if I can do it again," he said breathily.

"No need," the old man said.

Dave's eyes jerked up and the old man was smiling. He pointed up into a slanting cut between the rocks. "That's the top," he said. "Now if we can just foot it another twenty miles, we're there."

TWENTY-FOUR

Following the riverbed, Seth and Dave pushed into the plateau.

The wind came harder now, careening across them, rushing over the high, more level land.

Dave didn't know what was keeping him going, much less the old man. How the hell does he do it? he wondered. Seth never seemed to tire.

They wound along the river until it began to curve, then Seth led, slogging up the bank and over the edge.

"Line of low hills," he said, pointing. "They'll take us into Grass River."

Dave tried to see what he was talking about, but it did no good. The blowing snow obscured everything.

Without saying anything, Dave started walking again. He had only gone a few steps when he felt his knees giving under him. Sitting down in the snow, he watched the old man moving away from him. He looked up, trying to say something, but his voice came out a moan.

Rest, he thought. Just a minute, just a—

Suddenly Seth was in front of him.

"Tired," he cawed, "I'm—"

"Get up," the old man ordered.

"Minute," he whispered. "Minute."

"Get up," the old man growled again. "You're givin' up, boy. Now get up."

Anger twisted in Dave's throat. "Not . . ." he murmured, and raised his voice. "Not givin' up . . . tired . . ." He put out his hand. "Help me."

The old man shook his head and knelt down. "You're lettin'

it beat you, son. If you want to live, then you're gonna have to get your butt up out of that snow and walk out of this damn place. On your own."

The anger surged through Dave. Almost independent of him, his feet and hands began to move, pushing under him, straining, then shoving him up.

Wavering, he stood.

And walked.

Waiting, Ann could feel the night in the wind.

Turning across the porch, she walked back into the courthouse and the room being used as a headquarters. Fred Tolliver sat at the table in the middle of the room and Quade was at the stove, pouring a cup of coffee.

He looked around as Ann entered. "Coffee?" he asked.

"Yes." She nodded and sat down at the table.

"Wind lettin' up any?" Tolliver asked her.

She shook her head. "Afraid not."

Carrying the cups to the table, Quade joined them.

The sheriff stared at his cup for a second, then pushed his hat back, sighing. "Maybe I'd better go see to the boys. Take 'em a little of this."

Frowning, the patrolman looked across the table at Quade. "Tom," he began, "I hate to say it, but—"

"I know." Quade nodded. "I'm beginnin' to believe we ought to give it up too." He glanced at his coffee distastefully. "Why is it there's never nothin' around on a stakeout but coffee? You know what I'd give for a cup of chocolate. . . ."

He was pushing away the cup when the door burst open and a young patrolman rushed in.

"Lieutenant," he said to Tolliver, gasping for breath, "I'm not sure, but I'd swear I just spotted somethin' out there and . . ."

He was still talking as Quade exploded out of his seat and was running with Tolliver and Ann following.

TWENTY-FIVE

Seth smelled the town first. Smoke and people and horses.

"Dave," he whispered urgently. Grasping the younger man's shoulder, he pointed to the top of a rise in front of them. "Up there . . ."

The two men ran-crawled, stumbling up the incline, topping it. Below them the disjointed shapes of buildings hovered vaguely in the blur of snow.

"We did it!" the old man said thankfully, sitting down in the snow. "Damned if we didn't do it."

Dave nodded and, slumping down beside the old man, raised his eyes to try and see the high country. It was lost in the twisting whiteness.

His eyes dropped to the town. The slope fell away under him into the buildings wandering among the hills. The town rose and fell with the hills. Halfway down the slope Dave could make out the beginnings of a road.

And down the road he saw the men.

His eyes jerked to Seth. He had seen them, too.

"Son," he began.

"Sorry, old-timer," the young man whispered; and twisting, he brought up his fist, taking it across the old man's face. The impact stunned him, tumbling him down on his back.

Dave's eyes locked on the Henry for an instant and, shaking his head, he turned, plummeting over the rise and down the slope before Seth could get to his feet.

Twisting in the snow, the old man blinked, pulling himself up. "Damnit . . ." he growled.

Running, Dave slammed down through the snow, tripping,

then tumbling, crashing through a wad of brush and into the road. He scrambled to his feet and limped across the road, then down the bank and between a pair of old, leaning shacks. Hesitating, he looked back up the hill.

Seth was on his feet, stumbling to the edge, taking his rifle from his shoulders.

Pivoting, Dave ran away from the road to the back of the shacks. The town lay before him in a mangled twisting of hulks. Squinting, he could see the highway and, beyond it, the ridge.

And then the trees.

He could feel them now.

The sound of Seth's clamoring down the hill pushed him on. Across open ground. Between more shacks. Into another road.

He turned to use the road down the hill when he saw the uniformed man at the bottom of the hill.

Charging across the road, he ran between a ruined chicken house and a fence.

Up the hill, Seth pushed down the embankment, through the buildings, and out into the dirt street.

"Seth."

Turning, the old man saw Tom and Ann running toward him.

"Annie?" he said. "What the hell—?"

"You see him?" Quade cut him off.

"Off in there." Seth pointed down the hill.

"He armed?" Quade asked.

"No," the old man answered, and was running again.

Dave plunged around the side of a house, nearly colliding with a skinny patrolman, a rifle across his shoulder.

"You—" he sputtered.

Before the patrolman could do anything else, Dave ducked his shoulder, ramming it into the patrolman's bony ribs, sending him sprawling backward. The rifle exploded next to Dave's ear as they both tumbled into the snow.

Air whooshed out of the patrolman in a raking moan as the wind was crushed from his lungs. Struggling for breath, the patrolman's hand closed on Dave's arm. Trying to stand, Dave shoved him back, making the hand grip tighter, dragging down the fugitive.

Twisting, Dave swung his free hand into the patrolman's arm, breaking the hold. The patrolman crunched back into the snow, air scraping through his mouth.

Dave stepped back, then, bending down, picked up the rifle.

"Hey," the patrolman sobbed, then shouted, his voice gaining strength. "Hey!"

The rifle in hand, Dave fled down the street.

Behind him, the patrolman rolled over, fumbling his pistol from its holster. Cocking it. Stretching out his arm.

Dave rounded the corner of a house as the slug chopped away a chunk of wood.

Hearing the shot, Seth reeled down the dead buildings, Ann and Quade with him, charging through a yard and across a broken fence into another street. Seeing the downed patrolman, he ran to him.

"You all right?" Seth asked, kneeling down.

The patrolman managed to sit up, his eyes still wide from the lack of air.

"Guess," he wheezed raggedly. "Bastard took my rifle. You know how much a Winchester costs."

"That tears it," Quade spat.

The rattle of hooves jerked up Seth's eyes. He stood as a man rode in on a wiry roan.

Seth looked to Quade. "He's not a killer, Tom."

"I haven't got the time," Quade snapped, and looked up at the horseman. "Bring him down," he ordered him.

Ann pushed between them. "Mr. Quade, please. You said I could try—"

"It's too late for that," the sheriff said. "We've run out of options."

Reaching out, Seth grasped the reins of the horse.

"Hold on," he said to the man on the horse, then turned to Quade. "That the way it is?"

"That's it."

"Then I'll bring him down," the old man said. "I can do it without killin' him."

"Seth," Ann pleaded.

"It's the only way," the old man growled, and looked to the man on the horse. "I need your animal a spell."

The horseman raised his eyes questioningly to Quade, and Quade nodded.

"Do it," he said.

The man on the horse dismounted and Seth swung into the saddle, turning the animal out, running him.

In a deserted house one street down, Dave watched Seth come around a building, then eased away from the window.

"Him and his goddamn reward," he growled tightly.

Carrying the rifle, he crossed the room quickly and rushed out the door, then down the hill toward the main part of town.

He crouched beside an old fence.

Below him was a barn and corral, and beyond them the main street of town. There was a police car on it in front of the old courthouse.

Frowning, Dave sighed. He was going to have to go wide.

The sound of voices up the hill jerked him up and he moved. Skirting along the fence, keeping low, he edged down the hill. Across an open space into the barn. He rushed down the aisle of the barn to the far door. Above him the wind ached in the old boards. Looking up, he could see the old planks trembling.

Leaning against the frame of the door, he looked down on the main street. The car was still in front of the old courthouse. Exhaust smoke punctuating the snow. A figure moved beside it.

Dave jerked back into the barn.

Turning, he ran back to the other door.

The rattle of horse's hooves stopped him. His eyes moved frantically over the barn and, seeing a side door, he ran for it, easing it open and slipping outside into the corral.

Keeping low, he ran along the barn to the fence, then turned and followed it across the hill. At the end of the fence he stopped, frowning. He was moving away from the ridge. He needed to be going in the other direction.

A hulk congealed out of the snowfall at the other end of the fence.

"Halt," a voice shouted.

Dave bolted. Keeping the fence between him and the figure, he skidded down the hill toward the main part of town.

A shot crashed behind him. Then another. He kept running, making it to the edge of the buildings and into an alley.

Deep into the alley, he stopped.

He was being forced directly toward the patrolman he'd seen with the car.

Hesitating, he listened. Someone was coming down the side of the courthouse. Dave slipped back the way he'd come to a low, brick building next to the courthouse, then squeezed between it and a shack and turned toward the main street.

Coming to the head of the building, he saw the patrol car again. Easing his head out, he couldn't see anyone around it. The car was empty.

Keeping the heater going, Dave thought, his eyes combing the street.

Boots scraped the alley. Probably the man that belonged to the car.

He heard the man in the alley again.

Dave swore softly. He had to move. He had—

His eyes fixed on the car. Without thinking about it again, he broke from the buildings, running for it.

"Down here," someone shouted from the alley.

Dave slammed into the fender of the car, then rounded it, jerking open the door. He threw in the rifle, then followed it. It was deliciously warm inside.

"Jesus," he sighed. Then, seeing a uniform emerge from between the buildings, he jammed the car into gear.

The car leapt forward and, twisting the wheel, Dave floorboarded the gas pedal, fishtailing in the middle of the street, bringing the car around toward the highway and the ridge beyond.

Swinging the car straight, Dave hit the gas, exploding through the snow, careening through an old hitching rack, shattering it, then glancing off a porch back into the street.

Below the barn, Seth saw the car racing up the hill.

"Nate," he shouted to the horse before he thought. The horse jumped beneath him and, stretching out, hammered down the hill and up the main street.

Giving the roan his head, the old man turned him up between the old stores, trying to cut off Dave. The old man could hear the scream of the motor and the grinding of tires as Dave maneuvered a corner, then burst down the highway and across it, shooting up a road toward the ridge.

The old man clattered across the pavement and up the street parallel to the route Dave had taken.

Coming up the hill, the old man jumped a fence and then another.

On the hill above the barn Quade, Ann, and a young patrolman stopped, watching the two men.

"Jesus," the patrolman whispered amazedly. "Look at the old bastard ride. . . ."

Seth spurred the roan along the houses and into the street just in front of the speeding car.

Dave jerked the wheel around to avoid Seth as he darted into the road. The momentum swept the rear of the car around, sliding it through the snow. Twisting around, Dave saw the side of a house rushing toward him. He tried to bring the car around but the trunk plummeted through the corner of the house, buckling metal and exploding rotting wood through the rear window.

As he hit the house Dave jammed down on the gas pedal again, crashing through a porch support and back into the street.

Turning the roan, Seth charged back toward the car.

Dave saw the old man bearing straight at him. Twisting the wheel, he swerved into a yard, plowing through snow and mud.

The tires rammed into the soft ground, spinning themselves down into it, chewing to a halt.

Silence.

Dave hit the gas. The tires spun deeper into the mud.

Crimping the wheel and angling the tires, Dave shoved it into reverse. Off to one side, he could see the old man swinging around. Dave tapped the gas, rocking the car back, then again, giving it gas as he rolled back. Still going backward, he bounced up and out of the trough he'd dug. Stomping the gas, he backed around the old man, rattling into the street.

He hit the brakes.

The old man was turning. Trying to cut him off again.

Dave pulled it into drive, punching the gas pedal.

The old man kicked the roan, rushing in at an angle.

Dave edged to the far side of the street. Seth plunged in on him. Plowing off the road away from the old man, Dave held it straight, crushing a picket fence and bursting into another yard. The old man was still with him. Dave pounded into a high cross street. The shocks closed, slamming into the car, vaulting it up, sailing over the street, down a steep side, careening down the hill.

He was gaining on the old man. Dave turned the car back toward the road, giving it all the gas it had. He crashed back on to the street in front of the old man and, fishtailing, gained more on him.

Bringing his eyes around front, Dave saw the ridge ahead of him. Over one more hill. The engine screamed, pulling the slope, slipping on ice off to one side, hitting soft ground.

Dave swung it back into the middle of the road and up over the crown of the hill. The speed and the sideways motion of the car sent it into a slide down the hill into a curve, slamming to a sudden halt against a rock.

Kicking open the door, Dave grabbed the rifle and ran. Stumbling down the hill, then up the face of the long ridge.

Seth topped the hill. He saw the car first. Then Dave going

over the crest of the ridge. He pulled his rifle up as Dave dropped over the edge.

The roar of engines pulled his eyes around. Two patrol cars were racing toward him.

"Hup," he barked, and the horse pounded down the hill and up the ridge. Pushing over the edge, Seth hauled in the roan, searching the blurring white for Dave. Two hundred yards away were the trees.

He spotted Dave more than halfway across the clearing between the timber and the ridge.

Dismounting, Seth levered the Henry.

Running, Dave tripped, slamming to his knees, his breath raking through him. He pulled himself up and stumbled. Trying again, he fell.

He raised his eyes to the trees.

On the ridge, Seth heard the patrol cars grind to a halt below him. Quade and the patrolmen were starting up the ridge. Ann was behind them.

Seth looked back to Dave, still on the ground, the line of trees and the mountains beyond.

Those damned mountains.

The old man raised his rifle. Sighting down it. Holding his breath to steady his shot. Squeezing the trigger.

He put one an inch from Dave's hand. The next just below his feet.

Dave jerked up. Another shot plumed the snow next to him and, stumbling, shoving himself to his feet to run, he looked back to see where the firing was coming from.

He saw the old man on the ridge. He had a dead bead on him.

Straightening up, Dave turned, facing him.

The rifle stayed on him a moment, then nosed down, slipping away from Seth's shoulder, easing down to hang at his side.

Nodding, Dave McCord lifted his hand; then, turning, he began to run for the trees.

"Now find that cabin," the old man whispered.

Beside him Quade scrambled over the top with Tolliver and two other men. Ann was just below them.

"There." The sheriff pointed to the running man.

"No," Ann screamed, coming over the rise, but the patrolmen were already firing at the running man as he plunged into the trees.

And was gone.

The patrolmen lowered their rifles.

"He made it," Ann whispered in the echo of the shots. "He really made it."

Quade stared unbelievingly at the trees for a moment, then ripped off his hat and slammed it to the ground.

"Goddamnit," he raged. Pivoting, he glared at Seth. He started to say something, then held it, trembling. Reaching down, he picked up his hat.

"Want us to go after him?" Tolliver asked.

"You know the country?"

Tolliver shook his head wearily. "Afraid not."

"Anybody?" Quade asked, and when no one answered, he nodded. "Then he's won." He looked at Ann. Then back to Tolliver. "You'd be lost in ten minutes. Might as well go home," he sighed. "All of us."

Tolliver and his men turned down the slope and Quade looked to Ann.

"Ready?" he asked.

"Yes." She nodded and began to follow the patrolmen.

Tom's eyes moved to Seth. Still staring at the trees.

"Go on," the sheriff said to Ann, and stepped back to the old man.

As Ann started down, Quade fixed his eyes on Seth.

"You lost it all," he said.

"Maybe not," the old man said, more to himself than the sheriff. Then, raising his eyes, he smiled. "I can still work, and there's this." He held out the Henry to Quade. "You're always tellin' me how damn valuable it is."

"Seth . . ." Tom protested.

"Just a rifle." The old man swallowed, pushing it into Quade's hands.

Quade looked at it, then shook his head wearily, frustrated. "If you'd just stopped that damn fool—"

"No," Seth cut in, "he's not a fool. A hundred years ago he'd've been one to ride the river with."

Quade frowned gently. "A hundred years ago." He nodded. "But like you said, those days are gone."

"The days," the old man allowed, mounting the roan, "but maybe not the men."

In the saddle, his eyes lingered on the line of trees for a moment; then, tugging the horse's head around, he eased him over the side, descending back toward town.

Quade's eyes softened as he watched the old man.

"No, Seth," he said quietly, "not the men." His hand tightened on the Henry and he started down the slope. "Not the men. . . ."